JUST *for* MERCY

Mercy Series – Book 1

JUST *for* MERCY

Hannah Ngozi Chukwu

JUST FOR MERCY
Copyright © 2016 by Hannah Ngozi Chukwu

This is a work of fiction. Names, characters, places and incidents either are the product of the author's imagination or are used fictitiously, and any resemblance to actual persons, living or dead, businesses, companies, events, or locales is entirely coincidental.

Unless otherwise indicated, all Scripture quotations are taken from the King James Version of the Bible.

Printed in Canada

ISBN: 978-1-4866-1184-3

Word Alive Press
131 Cordite Road, Winnipeg, MB R3W 1S1
www.wordalivepress.ca

MIX
Paper from
responsible sources
FSC® C016245

Cataloguing in Publication may be obtained through Library and Archives Canada

DEDICATION

To the God of my Mercies, may this be a first-fruit offering to bless the world.

To my mother, Mrs. Mercy Umeakanne, the fearless supporter of my late father in the ministry, the wise model leader of young women and dedicated teacher. Your life has taught me faith in action, generosity and kindness without seeking for gain.

To the memory of the late Dame Fanny Ekpunobi, who was a mother to my husband and me. Your works still bring you praise as you continue to rest in heaven.

To all women who are builders even when not recognized. The pages of this book tell your stories.

CONTENTS

ACKNOWLEDGEMENTS

It takes a community to create a thing of value and beauty. There aren't words to show my appreciation adequately. However, I pray individuals will be able to see beyond the limitation of my words to the heart of humble gratitude for all the support, help, and inspiration I received in the process of creating this book.

First, I acknowledge the God of my Mercies for being my first and foremost encourager and inspiration through the Holy Spirit. He poured grace upon grace on me and again and again proved to be my Father indeed. I pour out my thank offering and say, "Thank You, Lord, for being such a faithful father-friend and loving me enough to let Jesus die for me so that I can have options and examples in this life." To Jesus, my Savior and Lord, for being the friend that sticks closer than a sibling and makes my yoke easy and my burden light.

I thank Reg Pope, who recognized in me the gift of creativity and so paid for me to go to Bowen Island for a writing course through Regent College in Vancouver. This book was birthed there on that island. God will bless you continually for your thoughtfulness in sowing a priceless seed in my career as a writer.

I thank my husband, Rev. Kingsley I. Chukwu, Ph.D., my faithful partner and able leader for his support and encouragement. I appreciate his vision that I could be a writer and excel at it. Kingsley, I appreciate your untrammeled support and sacrifice when I resigned my job to pursue my passion. You bring out the best in me. I love you.

I thank my children, Nobleman, Chimdalu, Idinakachukwu, and Chidiebere for their understanding and prayers. I thank them for sharing in the pain of separation with understanding and hope that it will help work out something better for the family. You are great children and very special to me. You shall do great things in this life. I am proud to be your mother and I love you to pieces.

I thank my brother, Prof. J. C. Umeh, for his inspiration and prayers. I thank my sister, Mrs. Kenechukwu Ohagim, for being my best friend and sister and for constantly praying for me to succeed in whatever I lay my hands upon. I thank my brother-in-law, Engineer Onyeudo, for his staunch support and cheerleading. I thank my sister, Mrs. Esther Iheme who shared part of the story with me. I appreciate the love and faith my siblings have in me to do great things. I thank you all for instilling in me confidence in who I am.

I thank my friend Sally Meadows for her encouragement, support, and example in the area of writing and publishing. She introduced me to Word Alive Press and was willing to walk alongside as a guide.

I thank Micky Wilkinson for reading through the manuscript and offering suggestions. I thank my international friendship partners Doreen and Glenn Stumborg for their friendship. I thank Doreen for reading part of the first draft of the book and encouraging me.

I thank Hailee Friesen for taking my photo for the book cover. Your skill and talent will yet bless many people in this world.

I thank Jen Jandavs-Hedlin and Amy Groening of Word Alive Press for working with me through the process of publishing this book. Your gentle approach and insight have made the publication of this book possible at this time. I thank Evan Braun, my distinguished editor. I enjoyed working with you. Your experience and expertise inspired me to expect and to receive nothing but the best for the work.

I thank my friend, Prof. Janice Fiamengo, for taking me under her wings as a friend and as a Christian sister. She mentored and nurtured my love for literature and writing. I cannot forget you, Janice, for the selfless love you poured into me and my family.

I thank all the individuals who supported me through their prayers. To my numerous friends and well wishers, I give my thanks. You all contributed to the success of this work through your kind words and joy at seeing this work become a reality.

INTRODUCTION

Just for Mercy is about diverse human experiences. These experiences may be different, but in the cultural context of the characters that have them, they have a thought-provoking verisimilitude. However, even though the episodes took place in Nigeria, not everyone would have had such experiences or believed them exactly. Nonetheless, these experiences demonstrate sensitivity peculiar to individuals who are not just religious but spiritual, too.

Spiritualism is becoming a welcome bedfellow in literature to help us understand the power of the human soul, especially in regards to the intimate interconnectedness amongst the spirit, soul, and body. The ability of the human spirit to perceive, tap, and articulate realities so as to transcend our physical limitations and unite us as spirits living in a physical world fosters wholeness and connectedness among communities. The author has chosen these episodes in order to illustrate the fact that the spiritual and physical world are interrelated; therefore, in order to achieve a holistic experience of life, one needs to understand the resultant impact of one on the other.

The characters exude confidence and skill in dealing with both the spiritual and physical worlds, leaving no room for fear, superstition, or intimidation, as is often the case when dealing with unknown or non-physical worlds. The motif of people being attacked by Satan and deceived with evil, or blessed by God and helped by angels, is classic and abounds in most literature, whether ancient or modern. Life challenges come in different forms and degrees; each form—whether spiritual, mental, emotional, social, political—is given a degree of emphasis to illustrate its role in the growth and impact individuals can experience. However, people's environments create the awareness and the understanding that will either help them to interpret their experiences, or make them ignore such experiences or suggestions as meaningless, irrespective of the fact that they may experience some interesting phenomena in their lives.

To publish this kind of story in Africa or North America, to be read by the public, behoves the audience to do one of two things: to willingly suspend their disbelief and enjoy the story, or to outright disbelieve, but even in their disbelief read the story and interpret it in view of the characters who have the experiences.

At the end, the insight gained from the story about comradeship, the wisdom to be resolute in fighting any battle, the power of choice in determining one's destiny, and faith are applicable to everyone, irrespective of their cultural environment.

CHAPTER ONE

Keziah is a widow of fifty-five years. She is a strong-built woman, six feet tall, and is physically vigorous, with broad powerful hands, and fair in complexion. A flat nose, punctuated by a well-rounded tip, marks her round face. Her high cheekbones and gentle eyes give her the look of nobility. She is often described as a woman with a heart of gold. Mama Joe lost her husband when she was pregnant with Jonathan, her fifth child. She has come a long way in her struggle on behalf of her family. The economic life of her family has much improved. Though Joe, her first son and third child, was only six years when his father died, Keziah's industry and wisdom have made him socially and economically better off than most boys who still have both parents alive.

Mama Joe, as a young girl growing up in a village, was known as *nwoke-nwanyi*. She is considered to be both a man and a woman in a single personality. Girls in her age group used to claim that the reason she is very strong is because her radius and ulna are combined into one. They describe her as the single-boned woman. Mama Joe used to beat both male and female members of her age group in any fight.

When Keziah was twenty-three years old, she married Odiba Aneto, who was fifteen years older than she was. Although Odiba loved and respected his wife, he was often disturbed by the fact that they were not able to have a child. In their culture, Keziah, as a woman, was blamed for the lack of children. Odiba's relations and friends pressured him to marry another wife. Sometimes they taunted him as being Keziah's houseboy, not her husband.

Odiba was unable to bring himself to marry another wife for many reasons: Mama Joe was a very hard-working woman whose work contributed much to the financial wellbeing of the family. Odiba was a conscientious man and understood that bringing in another woman as a wife would create a rival for Keziah and bring distractions to the family's goal of becoming financially self-sufficient. Because the couple grew close, Odiba wasn't convinced about keeping a mistress outside, as some of his friends suggested to him. He loved and trusted Keziah.

———

Even though Odiba thinks nothing is wrong, medically, with him or his wife, he consents to seek medical advice. His action provokes the ire of his friends, who barrage him with myriad criticisms: "That woman must have bewitched you so that you go to see a doctor with her. Since when did men consent to see doctors when their wives are barren? Perhaps Odiba is not even a man and has not performed his duty enough to get her pregnant." They feel sorry for him. He is contemptible, they think, and setting a bad precedent for other men whose wives will hear the story and require their husbands to seek medical advice in similar situations.

The doctor declares Odiba and Keziah medically fit and able to have children on their own. That gives them temporary relief, but their challenge does not go away completely. It hangs over them like a thick cloud, threatening to end their happiness—and even their marriage.

In the eleventh year of marriage, their first child, Nwakaego Esther (nicknamed Ego), is born to their great joy and relief. Finally, they are able to relax and have peace from some of their neighbours, who have been sneering and mocking them silently for years with contemptuous looks and sly innuendoes.

Now that Keziah's fertility has been proven, she and Odiba decide to make the business of raising a family their priority. By the time Nwakaego is a year and seven months, their second child, Judy Ifeyinwa, is born. A double joy, indeed, though they both wish she were a boy.

Another kind of struggle begins for Odiba. Just like most Nigerian men, he longs to have a male child to bear the family name. His medical training as a pharmacist makes him understand that having a male child is not entirely his wife's responsibility. This time, he is worried at his own inability to have a male child. He consoles himself by hoping that they may still have a male child. After all, was he not his parents' eighth child, with seven girls before him? He resigns himself to living peaceably, contentedly, and patiently with his wife. Much more, he learns the peace that comes from being thankful for what he has.

Six months after Judy's birth, Odiba is laid off his pharmacy job at the General Hospital in the city of Bida. He is fifty-two years old. They return to their hometown, the village of Ludu, because Odiba is unable to find another pharmacy job at his level. Keziah has to give up her thriving bakery business. They resign themselves to their lot and seek to make the best out of the situation. Life in the village is tough.

Odiba decides to set up a private pharmacy store and dispensary in their home. Luckily for him, he has a house he can call his own. Thanks to Keziah's foresight, they built this house while they were still living in Bida. As they were building it, people wondered why they would build such a big house when they had no children. People's provoking questions, disdainful looks, and insinuations threatened to end the project altogether if not for Keziah's resolute determination to carry on. At one point, Odiba refused to go home anymore to supervise the work because he was tired of questions.

Some people remarked that he was building a house for lizards, wall geckos, cockroaches, and rats to live in, as he had no children. Some even asked him if he just wanted to build a house where people could stay when they came to bury him. He was very discouraged, but Keziah reminded him, "People will always talk and you cannot stop them. That is the beauty and evil of community life."

Keziah took over the supervision of the building, and she never discussed with Odiba what people said or did around her in relation to the house. Perhaps they knew better to save their energy than to speak to a brick wall. The work was completed and it became one of the most modern houses in town.

When Keziah and Odiba move into the house, they are comforted by its luxury: a walled property they can call their own.

Unfortunately, their attempts to make a living through their home pharmacy is stalled by debt, as Odiba's patients owe him for the services he renders to them as well as for the drugs. They fold up the business, which brings little solace to them as Keziah is unable to start her side business of fashion and design; Odiba's business venture has drained all the family savings.

In the midst of this, the couple has another joy added to them. A baby boy is born two years after they return to Ludu. At last, Odiba feels fulfilled as a man. He is no longer anxious about anything. If he were to die, he would have no regrets. They name the boy Joseph Afamefuna (nicknamed Joe).

The family finds it difficult to make ends meet. They are scraping by. As soon as Joe is two years old, Keziah has no option but to take up farming. She is a woman who puts her whole being into anything she sets out to do and often outperforms everybody in doing so. She opts for large-scale farming. Her husband helps a little bit, but he is limited by his age and frequent asthma attacks. The burden of running the farm inevitably rests on Keziah, because she is younger and has the advantage of strength. In order to meet demand, they hire labourers to cultivate and plant the crops. Keziah takes responsibility for the weeding of the farm. She goes to work on the farm with a lantern so as to get work done before daybreak when Odiba is able to join her. Both of them want to avoid staying out too long when the sun is very hot.

One day when she's up working at 6:00 a.m., a viper bites her right hand. She is able to kill it and immediately leaves for home. By the time she gets home, the poison has spread through her body. She survives the poison but loses flexibility in her right hand for a long time. With that, she gives up on the idea of working on a farm with a lantern. Odiba is a renowned pharmacist; hence, he is not used to farming and it has never been his forte. They have to fold up their farming enterprise altogether.

Life becomes difficult again. With three young children to feed and other financial demands, Keziah and Odiba decide that it's time to try something else. They decide to borrow money from Keziah's brother in Lagos. With the money, they set up a poultry farm and begin to make some profit. To their joy, their fourth child, Obianujunwa Edith (nicknamed

Uju), is born three years after Joe. With more mouths to feed, and Odiba's failing health, Keziah decides to add a bakery shop to the poultry farm so that Odiba will be able to participate and contribute to the building of the family business without straining his health.

She begins to bake and sell confectionery goods, specializing in bakers' confections. Most times she just takes her products to give away at housewarmings, naming ceremonies, traditional marriage ceremonies, and the New Yam Festival. Soon people's interest in her bakery grows, and the demand begins to grow for her gourmet breads and fresh hot cakes. She receives orders for her baked products to celebrate weddings, birthdays, naming ceremonies, and anniversaries. She also begins to cater for these events. She always adds little extras for her customers, giving them more than they pay for. In spite of her generosity and overhead expenses, her business prospers within a year. She and Odiba then build a separate bakery with a fully furnished kitchen for the catering business. The family knows industry and discipline. They usually sleep at 9:30 p.m. and wake up at 5:30.

Keziah is seven months pregnant with their fifth child when Odiba's asthma attacks become too frequent. He dies at the age of sixty without seeing his fifth child.

The couple becomes known as Mama and Papa Joe, though Joe is the third child. Mama Joe is heartbroken and confused. She is unable to cry. The blow of the loss seizes both her voice and tears. Nwakaego is only eleven years old and Mama Joe almost loses the will to work.

During the seven-day burial and funeral ceremony for her husband, she finds it very hard to sleep. People say that she failed to sleep for the seven days because she refused to cry. Others say that it was because she wanted to be awake so as to converse with her deceased husband in the dead of the night.

Mama Joe is unable to eat, as she has no appetite. She rapidly loses weight to the extent that her friends and relations fear for her life. She becomes very sick with fever, notwithstanding being seven-month pregnant. She can hardly speak and people fear that she might die. Her relations are concerned because it is an abomination for a woman to die during the period of mourning for her husband. If the widow dies, it means that she killed her husband and that the spirit of her dead husband has taken revenge on her.

Even though Mama Joe is generally liked because of her generosity and is respected for her business, a few people still believe that she is queer, evil, and possibly a witch. Only through witchcraft could someone succeed in various business ventures without much struggle, they think. "What else? She must be a witch!" they gossip. If not for her respected position in town, her critics would make a case against her.

Some people are very upset that she is not subjected to a close questioning, even if it is just to humiliate her. Whether they are envious of her achievements and close relationship with her husband or concerned about her hurting other people, none of them are ready to admit.

CHAPTER TWO

Keziah's parents—her father Nwagbo and mother Mepe—also had a queer relationship. The couple was the talk of the town because of how close they were. One would not see one without the other.

One day Mepe, who was nursing Nwagbo from a bad cold, wanted to make a special herb soup for him with leaves of gongronema latifolium. Nwagbo, eighty years old, had not gone out with her to get the herbs from the garden. He had wanted to keep her company and take in some fresh air, but Mepe, seventy-five years old herself, convinced him to stay inside and rest. Most of the leaves on the gongronnema latifolium shrub were turning yellow, so she decided to walk to their farm; there were bound to be fresh ones there. She also wanted to check on the work done on the farm by their hired labourers since neither she nor her husband had been out there for one week. The farm was located close to the outskirts of the village.

A heavy downpour began twenty minutes after she left the house. She had nowhere to take shelter in the open field, so she kept going. By the time she gathered the vegetables and herbs and headed home, she had caught a bad cold.

Nwagbo was exhausted with worry by the time she came home shivering. Her health worsened from that incident and she was diagnosed with pneumonia. Every effort was made to help her recover, ranging from medical attention to traditional medicine and to herbal care.

During that time, Nwagbo greatly reduced his social interactions and mostly kept tender vigils at her bedside whenever he was free from domestic chores. He gave up his jovial and carefree attitude and became a grave man, no longer chatty and humorous.

After a year of slow but gradual progress, Mepe recovered, but she was unable to do any more hard work. It was a relief to their children and neighbours.

She managed though to live for another twenty-seven years, resting most of the time and never working in the gardens. Finally, three months after her one hundred and second birthday, she died on a Tuesday night. She was buried on Wednesday afternoon.

Nwagbo cried silently, and people saw only occasional tears drop from his eyes. In the night, after the burial of his wife, he called his children together to make his will known. He told his children that it would have been better for him to die in place of his lifelong companion. He firmly believed that if not because of Mepe's care for him, she would still have been living.

"I hope you know that my life is like the sun that had passed its setting time," he said. "Its sweetness and heat had been spent, but it only hangs on because of the sunshine and sweetness my late wife brought to it."

"What do you mean, Papa?" the eldest son, Matthew, asked, half teasing, half dreading the full meaning of his dad's statement. He was looking down so as to evade his father's gaze; his eyes would have betrayed his fear.

"Well, if you must hear it, I want to let you know that I cannot survive without my wife. I will follow her and we'll continue our lives together over there."

"No, Papa, you don't have to," Matthew protested. "You are still strong. Please stay a while with us. We need you."

He continued to discuss his final wishes with them, without any further reference to death or life. He maintained a resolute determination in his actions and words.

A week later, after the burial of his wife, on a Thursday morning, he seemed to look happier than he had in the past few days. His children sighed with relief as the dark cloud of their father's grief seemed to diffuse. *At last, our father has accepted to live,* his children thought.

However, Nwagbo went to bed that night never to sit again at the front of his piazza early to bless his household each morning.

The children buried him beside his sweetheart, his lifelong companion and lover. They made tombstones for these partners in life and death.

Young girls and boys would often sing about them in a love song:

You want to marry me
A bond, you'll die with me
We'll be Mepe and Nwagbo
Who tied the knot
Death could not untie
Our clan hears the stage is set.
We'll be lovers in life and death.

———

Keziah's friends fear for her life, having heard about the death of her husband, and then the death of her parents—but she is young, only forty-five years old, not even half as old as her mother by the time her mother died. Keziah's death would not be celebrated in a song; it would be remembered as a curse. While some are concerned, others deride her and spread rumours. Some people use excuses to pass by her house to see if she's still breathing or has tied the knot with her deceased husband.

After one month, she begins to show signs of returning to normal and recovering from absolute silence. She holds brief conversations with people. She visits her brother, Matthew, and her elder sister, Matilda, who both live in town. She keeps improving. She carries her pregnancy up to nine months and has a normal labour, delivering a baby boy, two months and two days after the death of her husband. The boy is named Jonathan Nnamdi.

She pulls through her queer silence, to the relief of her friends and relations, and gradually increases her outside activities. After a year of nursing her baby and mourning her husband, she begins to take cake orders again. She swings back into life. Her strange near-death sickness adds zest to her determination to get the best out of life while it lasts. It is as though the days of her mourning were like fertilizer, yielding more fruit for her future—as though her pain and sorrow are buried with her sickness, allowing a life of renewed strength to emerge. The energy and determination she exhibits seem to have doubled with her recovery. People are surprised at the degree of her increased industry and diligence, even in the absence of her husband.

Their amazement at her recovery, however, soon gives way to disdain and envy. Instead of respect for her diligence, some gossip that she communicates with the spirit of her dead husband through witchcraft and exchanges people's fortune for her own. Her near-perfect silence during the period of mourning is seen by some as a sign that she was communicating with the dead. Others think she has some supernatural abilities and may even be malevolent.

Meanwhile, she has gained some new friends and admirers who praise her for the industry of her hands. To them, a person's fate is ordained by their guardian spirit. However, most of the community believes that one can challenge and reject one's fate through hard work and diligence.

Her lifestyle lends credibility to all the opinions people have about her good fate and her faith, as demonstrated by hard work. She knows no fear and can face any danger. She works hard and hardly fails at any enterprise. Her hard work is like a wind dissipating her grief.

She gives up the poultry farm completely so as to focus on the bakery business, and she applies herself wholly to it. Keziah's business prospers as many people order wedding cakes from her, not only within Ludu but also from neighbouring towns and cities. Her cakes always taste delightful, her pastries delicious, and her food fresh. Her hard work and industry pay off again, for she comes to own the most successful confectionery and catering business in Ludu and environs.

Seven years later, she builds a large extension to the house for her business. Her five children become helpers; the older ones have become experienced professional caterers to the extent that Nwakaego, Judy, and Joe take contracts. They execute the contracts successfully with their mother's supervision.

CHAPTER THREE

Mama is the first to get up. She usually fetches water after having showered at the stream before dawn. She will sometimes go with a lantern or flashlight when the moon isn't up, but sometimes the moonlight gives her enough light to see the footpath. At dawn, she goes with her children to fetch more water to ensure they will have enough water for their day's work. They also end their day by doing one more round of fetching water.

One Friday morning in February, Mama wakes up. Without checking the time, she assumes it's already 5.00 a.m. She then takes her basin and sets off to the stream. The moon is very bright and clear. She notices that she's not meeting anybody along the footpath and wonders why; she's used to meeting at least three or five people, especially hunters and palm wine tappers coming back from their nightly enterprise. Being a fearless and independent woman, she continues towards the stream with brisk footsteps, focused on her mission.

From a distance, she notices a shiny flashing light. Once at the peak of the last hill before reaching the stream, she notices again, by the light of the moon, that the water seems troubled, as though some people are swimming in it. The low murmur of the waters and unusual ripples, almost rising like a tide, are steady and unrelenting. Others might have turned back at this point, but not Mama. She never considers turning back home without water in her basin. How would she compensate herself for the six kilometres she has already walked? She wouldn't even be able to explain what was unusual about the stream.

She has known this stream, Iyi, since she was a child. The only compromise she contemplates is to not bathe this time but just fetch water and go home.

By the time she's thirty-five metres from the stream, the water is calm and still. There is perfect silence. She feels relaxed as she gets to the edge of the stream. She breathes a deep sigh of relief, puts down her basin, and steps into the stream.

Just then, a significant wave, cresting five feet above the water, appears twenty metres away. Like a surprised lioness, curiosity takes over. She rubs her eyes and looks closely to make sure she's awake and not dreaming.

The wave approaches her with a raging force and knocks her over into the water. She's in distress but can't call anybody for help. By sheer strength of will, Mama doesn't faint and even manages to fetch her water and run back home.

Her children are still fast asleep. She finds it unusual that her children would still be asleep because they would normally be awake by the time she got back from the stream.

Things have been unusual today, she thinks.

When she decides to check the time, she is shocked to see that it is 2:30 a.m. She decides to go back to bed, but she has caught a fever.

At 5:30 a.m., her children find her still in bed. They know that their mother isn't one to be in bed so late. Nwakaego immediately senses that something is terribly and deeply wrong. She is convinced that something has dangerously fallen out of place in their home, but she is unsure about what it is—and afraid to find out.

CHAPTER FOUR

N
wakaego gently taps her mother's hand while the others stand around.

"Mama, are you all right?" The words freeze to her lips as she notices that Mama is shaking with fever and groaning with pain.

Mama makes no response.

Nwakaego repeats the question and then shakes her mother hard, out of alarm.

"I'm all right," Mama says in a shaky voice. "Please get me a cup of water. I went to the stream too early this morning and the waters were strangely troubled. I saw..." Her voice trails off and she's silent.

"The stream!" everyone echoes in alarm. They can only speculate about what has happened.

Nwakaego sends Uju to get the water.

All the children are present except Joe, who has travelled to Enugu to set up a wedding cake. Like terrified chickens before a ravenous hawk devouring their mother hen, they are incapable of running away from the reality starring them in the face. They are frozen with fright. They are helpless and unable to cry. From the youngest to the oldest, none can find their voice.

When Uju brings the water, they help their mother to sit up in bed. Nwakaego takes the cup from Uju and transfers it into their mother's shaky hand. Mama spills the water on the floor and is unable to bring the cup to her lips. Nwakaego reaches out and takes the cup from her.

It is alarming to think that their mother, who could normally lift a fifty-kilogram bag of flour with ease, is now suddenly so sick that she cannot hold a cup of water. The sight of her struggle breaks their resolve. In unison, they burst into tears. They clutch one another and begin to weep and shout. They feel their world collapsing before them. Even the youngest, ten-year-old Jonathan, seems to understand what's happened, and he cries loudest of all.

For the first time, they see tears roll down Mama's cheeks, something that didn't even happen when their father died. The sight scares them and makes them feel as if the ground has opened its mouth to swallow them up. Their mother is like a piece of solid ground they have been standing upon all these years. Their defence against the challenges of life is disappearing before their very eyes. The evil wind that their mother has withstood on behalf of the family has been let loose in all its fury. Their mother, their strength, their succour and guide, who fears neither human nor spirit, is being destroyed.

Nwakaego immediately assumes the responsibility that has fallen on her. She puts the cup against Mama's lips. Her mother drinks a little, then stops crying and relaxes her face to give Nwakaego a look of approval. She lies back in bed.

"Now, let everyone stop crying, please," Nwakaego says, mustering authority like a nervous preacher to a scattering flock. "Mama is still alive; she is not dead."

Her words are a reassurance that there is hope; their mother is still breathing. Meanwhile, she wonders about what to do next.

Mama looks at her with approval, but unable to utter a word. Catching her mother's eyes, Nwakaego is encouraged but the hopelessness of the situation seems too much for her.

"Judy, please go call Papa Sunday," Nwakaego instructs. "Ask him to come to help us take Mama to the hospital."

Papa Sunday, also known as Mr. Ignatus Abiazie, is a commercial bus driver. His nickname is Obododinma, and he usually leaves home early for his daily route, which run from Ludu to Enugu from Monday to Wednesday, then Ludu to Onitsha from Thursday to Saturday. He drives most weeks, except when the bus breaks down or he is unable to work due to weakness. He rarely falls sick or takes planned holidays.

Mama Joe raises her hand as Judy dashes off through the bedroom door. "Please don't call him…"

Nwakaego is encouraged to hear her mother's voice, but at the same time curious as to why she doesn't want them to get help. What mysterious sickness has suddenly seized her this morning?

She summons her courage. "Why don't you want us to call him? We need help. You don't feel well at all. Allow us to call him so that he can take you to the hospital.

"What do you think is wrong with me?" Mama asks, gathering her strength.

"I'm not sure I know, Mama, but you obviously don't feel well."

"I know, but… Papa Sunday can't help me."

"Ooh, Mama, please tell us what can help you."

Mama sighs. "Sleep left my eyes. I thought it was morning already, so I went to the stream. I was nearly drowned because of a strange wave."

"Oh Mama!" the children scream.

"I'm not sure any doctor can help me. The shock and lack of sleep have disorganized m—y bo—dy," she stammers painfully. They wait for her to say more, but she goes silent.

"Please, Mama, tell us what to do," Nwakaego pleads.

Mama still doesn't say anything.

They wait until Nwakaego assumes her leadership role again, and Nwakaego wishes she had the power to diagnose and treat this unusual malady. She spent only one semester at the School of Nursing and Midwifery in Mbia. She has come home on a vacation and wishes she had learned something that would be useful in her mother's present state.

Suddenly she remembers that her mother enjoys singing and listening to music.

She may need a therapy that soothes her nerves and gets her to relax so she can catch some sleep, she reasons. Music will soothe and calm Mama's agitated mind and help her recover from the traumatizing experience at the stream.

Nwakaego turns to the others. "Let's sing songs for her."

The songs diffuse the tangible silence, unuttered confusion, and distress that's taking over this once happy and confident family. They sing "Amazing Grace," then "The Blood of Jesus, God our Solid Rock" and

"Deep and Wide Fountain." They sing and sing until they are almost hoarse and can hardly think up any more choruses to sing.

The songs are a therapy for them as well. They become relaxed and seem to forget their sorrows momentarily. They even forget about the passage of time and the fact that they haven't yet had breakfast.

As their songs continue, Mama sleeps—opening her eyes once in a while but always closing them again. When it becomes obvious that they have run out of songs and are equally tired, the singing dwindles to a hum. Nwakaego then stops the singing altogether. Mama is sleeping deeply and her once drawn face seems relaxed.

"Let's leave her to sleep and maybe eat some breakfast," Nwakaego suggests.

Judy stays with her while Nwakaego, Uju, and Jonathan go to the kitchen to get breakfast ready.

After breakfast, Nwakaego assembles everyone for a consultation. She wishes Joe was home, but unfortunately he won't be home until Sunday, two days away. They have to find solutions before calling on neighbours to help. Mama doesn't like it when they involve outsiders in their problems.

"We must do something," Nwakaego says.

"But what shall we do?" Jonathan asks.

When no one answers, Nwakaego continues. "All right, I suggest that we all take her to the hospital. I think that if we all insist, she will consent."

Judy isn't sure that will work. They call her the deep one, for she is often seen sitting alone and gazing intently into vacancy with a bright look on her face, as though birthing some exciting ideas. She also understands Mama more than the others. In fact, on some evenings when the family sits together after a day's labour, she whispers things in Mama's ear. Others often wonder what she whispers about, but they don't feel worried or jealous. Mama is there for every one of them.

"Do you all agree?" Nwakaego asks. Uju and Jonathan nod. Nwakaego turns to Judy. "What do you think?"

The two sisters occasionally disagree sharply with each other on certain serious matters, but they usually make up without much fuss.

Today Judy is afraid to speak up; she knows that if she counters Nwa-kaego's suggestion, the responsibility to find a workable solution will fall on her. She is not yet prepared to shoulder that responsibility.

"I don't know," Judy says. "I'm wondering if we should let her sleep. Perhaps she will be able to speak with us when she wakes up."

"Do you think she'll be fine when she wakes up?" Jonathan asks.

Judy is encouraged by that question. "Maybe she needs some rest to help her get over the shock of her encounter at the stream."

They go back into Mama's room to see how she is doing. They see that she is deeply asleep.

"All right," Nwakaego says. "Let us wait until she wakes up. Then we shall know what next to do."

CHAPTER FIVE

Nwakaego organizes the others for their day's chores, working on the orders that came in previously from customers. None of them ventures to go to the stream. They manage with the water they have in the house. They take turns to watch their mother, but Mama continues to sleep until 5:00 p.m.

"She has opened her eyes," Uju announces excitedly to Nwakaego, running from their mother's room into the bakery shop.

They rush into their mother's bedroom, but, disappointingly, they find her eyes closed. They don't doubt Uju's observation; they just have to put a check on their excitement.

After thirty minutes, she opens her eyes again.

"I need water," she says to Jonathan, who is sitting at her bedside.

Jonathan runs to the veranda where the others are busy arranging orders for pickup late in the evening. "Mama is awake now with her eyes wide open," he screams in excitement.

Everyone abandons the task at hand and rushes to the bedroom in excitement.

By the time Jonathan returns with Mama's cup of water, she is already sitting up in bed. Jonathan hands her the cup and she puts it to her mouth and drinks almost half the water. Her children begin to touch her, holding her hands as though to pull her out of bed, but she gently pulls back from them. She lies down again and closes her eyes. They observe as she falls asleep.

Disappointed, they return to their chores. They take turns watching her again, but Mama is still asleep after supper. They pray and linger, but at 9:30 Nwakaego sends everyone to bed and takes over the vigil.

Nwakaego brings in her mattress and bedsheet to make her bed on the floor. That way, she will be at hand to help if need be.

She sits up on her mattress, observing her mother for a while. Moments later, Mama opens her eyes; rather than getting up, she lies still for some minutes more.

When she does sit up, Nwakaego rushes to embrace her. To Nwakaego's surprise, Mama responds to her greetings coherently.

"What time is it?" Mama asks.

Nwakaego goes into the parlour to look at the wall clock. "Twenty minutes to ten, Mama."

Nwakaego dashes into the corridor that leads to the other bedrooms. "Wake up, everybody!" she shouts. "Come! Mama is awake!"

Everyone comes alive with excitement and rushes to Mama's room.

Sleep and music turn out to have been the cure. She sits up in bed and converses with her children. She narrates the story about her encounter at the stream, telling them about how she was knocked over by a wave and nearly drowned. They listen attentively and without fear because their mother is calm and relaxed.

Mama recovers without going to the hospital, and her business continues to thrive. She decides to sink a borehole to ensure that they have a constant water supply and no longer spend time going back and forth to the stream.

One of the effects of her recovery is that she starts to deemphasize work. She gradually changes from being a workaholic to finding time to visit people and taking brief rests some afternoons. She values social interactions more than before. But has she changed her attitude towards work because she has become financially independent? At the end of the family's expenses, she still has cash left for savings.

Her fearlessness and independence give way to caution. She gives more thought to spiritual matters. Though a member of the local Anglican Church, until now she has only gone to church on the rare occasion when she didn't have much work. Her religion was her work, and generosity her motto. After her experience at the stream, she begins to go to church more regularly.

Mama is a good woman, everybody agrees. She finds more time to visit people than they visit her. She is not only a regular member of the church but also joins a committee set up by the Christian Association of Ludu to unite the churches and evangelize the town. The committee has the mandate to organize an interdenominational outreach before the end of 1992. The committee is to liaise with a Christian group in Lagos towards a four-day crusade to share the good news of salvation and deliverance.

Ludu has sixty-four thousand inhabitants, and these people aren't alone in their struggles to come to terms with the new wave of spiritual revival that swept the whole nation in the 1970s after the Nigerian/Biafra Civil War. The wave of Pentecostalism marks the more recent Christian spiritualism and ties into the people's spiritual quest for dominion over unruly forces. The people's spiritual taste buds are now so sensitive to manifestations of power that they look forward to any opportunity to demonstrate control over seen and unseen forces. Stories about dominion and power over vicious forces, especially during crisis, excite the community, but excitement turns to tension when the stories become reality.

The people plan to carry out an interdenominational Christian outreach program next August, despite the rainy season, because that is the most propitious time. Rain witch doctors will attempt to ruin the program by inducing rainfall during the program so that they, too, can brag about the superiority of their powers. The spiritual forces at loggerheads, engaging in conflict and creating tension, permeate the community as each party seeks to flex its spiritual muscle to intimidate, appease, or rally their cohorts to their course. It is time for the community to know who is the spiritual boss.

The committee's task is huge, but its members have been carefully selected to be respected members of their community. Mama is one of them, and her growing influence lends credibility to the program. Nobody besides her children knows about her encounter at the stream, but people notice the change she has undergone. People have become her focus, not work. Some people say that she has made all the money she could ever make, and therefore it is natural for her to begin noticing other people.

As Mama takes interest in people, younger women begin to take interest in her. They see her as a model of industry and virtue. People still do not understand the source or the meaning of the change that has come over her.

Caroline, Mama's neighbour, is one such woman. She watches with keen interest the change that has come upon Mama.

CHAPTER SIX

Circumstances in Caroline's life move her to begin to reflect hard and long on her vocation and to assess whether she needs to make a change. She begins to imagine experimenting with other vocations, besides trading. Previously, she hadn't considered herself capable of working in a similar field to Mama. She imagines how strange it may be for her to become one of Mama Joe's apprentices; however, she reasons that it's not an entirely bad idea if it'll help her family's financial situation.

For some time, Caroline has been deeply engrossed by the question of how to increase the capital for her small household supplies business. She has often mused upon the possibility of having a higher monthly cashflow.

Caroline and Onyema, her husband, do not consult at the shrine of Ogwugwu or go to church. They believe that they can get whatever they need just by thinking and working hard.

They lived in affluence when Onyema was involved in an import business. He used to import ready-made clothing and household goods from Taiwan and Hong Kong to sell to Nigerian wholesalers. They also ran four boutiques in Lagos for the cream of society in Ikoyi and Victoria Island. They also owned a custom-built home in Lagos. Onyema even mused with Caroline about establishing a textile business, but his key oversea business partner swindled him. Onyema and Caroline incurred heavy losses.

They further invested most of their savings to import goods, in an attempt to remain in business. Unfortunately, the government impounded imported goods at the Lagos wharf that year to encourage indigenous industries. They had no way of surviving this, as they had used their remaining savings to bribe officials for the release of the goods. It didn't work. Bankrupt and heartbroken, their only option was to drastically on expenses, including food.

They sold their house and shops in Lagos to raise money to offset their heavy debts. For two years, their condition didn't improve. Their only option was to return to their hometown, Ludu, to start a new life. They had built a beautiful two-storey house in their hometown, hence they had a place to return to. But they were to find their bankrupt life even harder to manage in the village.

Caroline has been dreaming and hoping that one day they may recover their life savings and the assets they liquidated in order to pay back the loan they'd taken to increase their import business. She has heard stories about money doublers, but she doesn't quite believe that one can be such a nincompoop to fall for such a scheme. She doesn't believe in magic. Nevertheless, she believes that it is possible for an unexpected good, out of the ordinary, to change her family's bleak financial future.

"I wouldn't mind falling into luck one day," she muses to herself. She is tired of living from hand to mouth and always having to scrape by.

She has great expectations, but the glass ceiling of her limitations seems impenetrable. She muses continually about having a sudden windfall.

"In this pro-modern community, with the conglomeration of traditional and modern marketing strategies, many things are possible," she says to console herself.

Angelina, another neighbour of Caroline's, is involved in a similar retail business. One day, she visits Caroline in order to share a concern about their business.

"I am worried about our petty-trading because it's no longer prospering," Angelina says as soon as she sits down on the two-armed, high-backed chair in Caroline's living room.

"It's very unfortunate," Caroline agrees. "My family depends on the little profit from this business. Most of the big businesses in Onitsha now deal directly with local retailers of similar products. I remember when I used to sell all my merchandise within a week and return to Onitsha to buy more. Right now, it takes two to three weeks before I'm able to buy more goods. I'm considering giving up this business to look for something else to do. I've been thinking of Mama Joe, who out of necessity and for the good of her family has set up her own independent bakery. Now she's quite rich."

"Do you notice the change that has come over her recently?" Angelia asks. "She visited us the other day."

"Yes, she visited us too. I'm wondering about how to propose that she hire me as one of her apprentices. That way I can learn the trade and set up my own confectionery business."

"Good idea, Caroline," Angelina responds simply. She would rather talk about the pressing issue on her mind, the reason she has come to visit in the first place. "Well, Mama Joe informed me that the Christian Committee Association of Ludu is going to plan a program that involves another Christian group from Lagos. The program will last for some days to give them the opportunity to pray for people who need blessings and power to overcome their struggles in life."

Caroline nods. "Yes, I heard about that. I haven't thought much about it. The program definitely isn't for me."

"Me neither. I won't attend such a program. God is in heaven and He will bless everyone. My husband and I still believe in God, but we don't go to church. We don't kill, we don't steal, and we don't plot evil against anyone. We still worship the deity, Ogwugwu, and sacrifice to him. The priest of Ogwugwu helps us to know what we should do to protect ourselves without committing sacrilege or desecrating the land by breaking taboos."

"Onyema and I haven't believed or worshipped anything all our lives, even when we were living in Lagos and had money," Caroline says. "We still don't believe in anything, so nothing has changed. We do not worship God. In fact, I think God doesn't need anyone to worship him. The fact is that He doesn't bother anyone, so why should we bother him?" Caroline pauses, sensing that Angelina doesn't buy her carefree spirit towards the matter of religion. "We were prosperous as our business thrived, until four years ago. Even though our prosperity was cut short, we don't think it's an indication that we need to be religious. It's true that we're only barely above poverty level now—my world of comfort has been shattered and I'm learning what everything costs—but why should we attend such a program as Mama Joe is busily advertising?"

Angelina studies her friend closely, wondering about the resolution Caroline and Onyema have taken against religion. They looked so affluent when they came home for a Christmas celebration some years ago, with great pomp and show, comfortable business tycoons from Lagos. Onyema had boasted during a drinking spree that he had become like a god himself, because he could get whatever he wanted.

Angelina decides to take her leave, for two reasons. First, Caroline and Onyema had surely heard many things about religion from better speakers than herself, yet they have remained adamant. What could she tell Caroline that would make her reconsider? Second, even if she decided to talk to Caroline about worshipping Ogwugwu, she Angelina didn't have anything to show for all the years her family had served Ogwugwu, except that they kept making endless sacrifices and running to the priest to find out about all the new and different things they had to do in order to prosper. Despite all that, prosperity had eluded them. They were still as poor as ever.

Angelina gets up, stretches, and bends over to straighten the folds on her wrapper. "I think I'll be leaving now. Let's think of what's best to do about our business. Maybe if we increase our capital, we can buy more varieties of goods, thereby attracting more customers."

"You are correct," Caroline enthuses. "I'll definitely work on your suggestions."

"All right, my sister, until later."

"You have done well by coming to share your thoughts with me." Together they walk to the gate. "Greet your family!"

CHAPTER SEVEN

Caroline and Onyema have been married for fourteen years and have three boys—Mathias, Michael, and Marcel. Mathias has gained admission to the Federal Government College in Enugu, and they need thirty thousand naira to pay his tuition and boarding fees by the first week of September. So far they have been able to save only ten thousand naira, so they decide to look for help as early as they can. They decide to ask Caroline's brother, Obinna Okito, for help. He lives in Onitsha and works with First Bank.

Caroline sets off for Onitsha at 9:00 a.m., boarding Papa Sunday's bus.

The drive to Onitsha passes without incident, though it takes two and half hours because of poor road conditions and traffic congestion. During weekdays, Papa Sunday likes to leave as early as 6:30 a.m., saving himself from the hustle and bustle of traffic.

Onitsha is a very busy commercial centre and has the largest market in West Africa. A local saying claims that only the courageous and clever will be able to go to Onitsha and come back without losing everything they have on them. Humans and spirits, as well as honest people and rogues, do business together at the Main Market. The market is often crowded, to the extent that people used to say that a handful of dust thrown in the air may find it difficult to land on the ground.

Caroline is used to going to Onitsha to buy her wares, but it's always a hassle. However, this Saturday morning she's excited. She isn't going to shop, but rather visit her brother. She is glad to be spared the usual troubles connected with the market—all the haggling, shuffling, shoving, and struggling to push through the crowd and still hold tightly to one's purse, and finally running to catch up with the barrow boys who convey one's goods to transporter vehicles at different bus terminals, all this through a thick crowd of rambunctious motorist and cyclists.

Upon arrival at the bus depot at 11:30 a.m., all the passengers disembark. Caroline tucks her handbag under her arm and hurries away like the rest of the passengers. Most of them intend to return to Ludu that same day; only a few will not. Papa Sunday usually departs at 3:30 p.m., so the passengers must conduct their business quickly.

As Caroline hurries away, a man walking behind her touches her shoulder. "Wait, madam. I have a message for you."

Caroline startles, then turns to face the man. "Yes, what is it?"

"I'm a businessman from Mbia," the man says, stretching his hand to Caroline.

Caroline does not take his hand, but gives him a thorough look from head to toe. He looks to be in his early forties, about six feet tall and dressed in a three-piece green suit with a matching tie. He carries a black leather briefcase in his left hand and a newspaper in the other, and he has a way of smiling with the corner of his mouth. Habitually, he rubs his right hand across his mouth as he speaks. He smells fresh and wears a well-groomed short afro, looking every inch an important gentleman in business.

He withdraws his hand and clears his throat. "Sorry to bother you, madam, but I must say that as soon as I saw you, I knew you were the right kind of person, suited for a business venture that's bound to yield profit quickly."

He gives a pregnant pause, weighing the effect of his words. Caroline is quiet and keeps looking at him without any facial expression.

"By the way," the man continues, "I'm an importer of hollandaise wax wrapper for wholesalers. I go to Hong Kong to buy clothes and then distribute them to middlemen who sell to retailers in different towns and villages." He stops abruptly. "Oh, I forget myself. My name is Mr. Aubrey Unna. How could I have kept you standing in this way? I usually sit down to discuss important business. Please, let's go over to that restaurant." He points to a place on the corner. "We shall discuss this over a soft drink."

Caroline doesn't move.

"I'm sorry for my presumption," Unna adds. "I hope you don't mind a bottle of Coke. I think you need it. You must be thirsty after your tiresome journey on that bad and dusty road."

Caroline's eyes never leave his face. She's studying him to make up her mind. What kind of person is this intruder? However, his undeniable courtesy convinces her not to walk away since.

On reaching a conclusion about him, she smiles. "No problem. I am interested in hearing about your business."

"Certainly. I know you are suited for this business. It is always said that we should trust our gut feelings."

He takes the lead towards the restaurant, which is only fifty metres down the road.

"My husband used to go to Taiwan and Hong Kong," Caroline says. "He imports ready-made dresses, cosmetics, and small household appliances."

Unna, frantically wracking his brain to keep her talking, quickly say, "Yes, I thought as much. You must be a lady with experience in the import business. I'm glad I didn't ignore my gut." He chuckles and Caroline smiles broadly. "If I may ask, what is your name?"

"Mrs. Caroline Okwueze."

Unna looks up suddenly, as though her name has stirred recognition in him. "It's nice meeting you, Mrs. Okwueze. I think your name sounds familiar to me."

Inside the restaurant, they seat themselves in the far corner, well separated from other customers. When a young waitress comes up to them, Unna asks Caroline to order her own drink—on him.

As soon as the waitress takes their orders and leaves, like a shrewd businessman, he eagerly resumes the conversation. "Tell me about your husband's import business."

"The business folded up because he was swindled by his long-time partner."

"I'm sorry to hear that," he says sympathetically. "What is your husband's name?"

"Onyema Okwueze, and we are from Ludu," she says, emphasizing *Ludu*. People from Ludu are widely accepted as wise and shrewd in business.

When the people of Ludu pulled down the missionary church there, the British government transferred their headquarters to Mbia. The British further showed their disdain by establishing a boy's secondary school in Mbia, as well as a school of nursing and midwifery, to provoke Ludu to envy and regret their resistance to "civilization." They viewed the people of Ludu as arrogant and uncooperative.

Ever since, Ludu and Mbia have fought a cold war. The people of Ludu often say that people from Mbia are saboteurs for yielding to British tactics. To boost their ego, they often say, "What is the Nmam stream of Mbia in comparison to Iyi stream of Ludu? If not for Iyi, there would be no Nmam, and therefore no Mbia."

"Now it has come together," Unna says, squeezing his brow and nodding his head as a wave of recollection sweeps over his brow. "I'm sure I must have met your husband on a business trip some years ago. You might ask him about me. He may likely remember me." With a look of sudden revelation, he adds, "This world is very small."

He shrugs his shoulders as Caroline watches.

"Now, let's continue our discussion, for it is meant to be," he says. "I'm very sure you are the right candidate to work with me. Oh, what a blessing to have such accurate instincts! Something in me directed me to stop you today. I live in Onitsha, but I go home to take supplies to my relations and business partners. I used to live in Lagos, but I decided to relocate. I consider it important to live close to home. I've been helping people gain more than they put into the hollandaise wax business. I offer good prices, making it easier for them to earn profits." He makes full eye contact with Caroline. "Are you willing to be my distributor in Ludu and the neighbouring villages?"

Without waiting for her answer, he continues, "You will make a lot of profit, because you'll collect the fabric at wholesale prices. You can sell each piece well above the wholesale price in order to make extra profit. This means that you'll make thirty-five percent off the cost of each piece you sell. You'll also earn a thirty-five percent commission off your total sales. Madam, you are bound to become rich within a short time. The retailers in the neighbouring towns may not even need to come to Onitsha to buy fabric anymore; you can sell to them. I'll make it even easier for you by bringing the wrappers to your home."

Caroline feels convinced that her dream of landing a good business has finally come true. "I'm willing to partner with you. How and when can we start?"

"We can start immediately. This is very good, madam. I will require you to make a deposit today, and I will bring the first consignment to you next week. I'm presently awaiting my goods from overseas. They are likely to arrive early next week on the ship—that is three days from now."

"I don't have any money on me," Caroline says.

Unna smiles broadly. "Oh no, please don't think I mean you must cover the cost of a whole twenty wrappers. You only have to make a starting deposit today. I will collect the balance after you've sold everything and deducted your profit, initial deposit, and thirty-five percent commission."

"Okay," Caroline replies with disappointment in her voice. "I have only my transport money back to Ludu. In fact, my reason for coming to Onitsha today is to borrow money from my brother to pay my son's tuition and boarding fees."

"Where does your brother live, and how much do you need to get from him?"

"Number Eight Nky Street, and I need twenty thousand naira."

"We can work something out," Unna says encouragingly. "Go to your brother and borrow the money for your son's school fees, and when you get back we'll discuss how I can supply the materials to you. One more thing, and it is very important: please don't tell your brother anything yet. He might discourage you, since he doesn't know me. He may not appreciate, at this stage, what you stand to gain from this business. It will be a pleasant surprise when you end up making so much money. I'll wait for you here. You see, I rent part of this restaurant as my office. Just ask anyone you find here about Mr. Aubrey Unna. They'll come tell me that you're back."

Placing his left hand upon his chest, he pulls up his shoulders and stands up. He adjusts his tie with both hands.

"Mrs. Okwueze, you are a very lucky woman. I am here to make you rich, for I am the Managing Director of Chief Aubrey Unna & Sons General Import and Export Ltd. You will be glad you met me today."

Caroline also stands up. With a smile, she says, "Thank you, Mr. Unna, I'll be back."

"All right, Mrs. Okwueze. I'll wait here for you."

CHAPTER EIGHT

S he takes her leave. As she continues down the block towards her brother's house, she reviews her encounter with Mr. Unna and wonders about how much money the man might want her to put down as a deposit. She would have liked to ask, but she could not bring herself to do it. She convinces herself that Unna, being very nice, might only want her to deposit one thousand naira at this stage.

She can already picture her economic power, rising like a tide. She imagines how she will announce her new business to Angelina. She might not need to become Mama Joe's apprentice after all. Through this new venture, she will make a lot of money. Her shrewdness and marketing skills are unbeatable. Her husband often compliments her about them.

Through the money she'll make, Onyema will be able to return to the import business again. But this time, she promises herself, she will work closely with him to ensure that they're not swindled again.

All the pleasures she has forfeited will be at her command soon. She will be able to prove the philosophy she and Onyema have always shared: that religion is nothing, and believing in yourself is everything.

She only hopes that her brother received the message they sent through one of their townsman last Saturday. Indeed, there will be no problem at all. Is she not destined to be successful and comfortable in this life? Have things not gone very well for her since she was born, except for the past four years?

She assures herself through these rhetorical questions.

Her brother, Obinna Okito, is a bank manager and lives in a modest duplex in one of the new areas of Onitsha. The house has twelve-foot wall with electrified top spikes. Such walls are standard safeguards in this area. They offer the rich a double protection against armed robbers.

She approaches the gate and presses the bell. A guard looks through a peephole embedded in the square window, covered by barbed wired and thick red glass. The window is close to the top of the gate that the guard can identify callers before revealing himself.

The guard, a man in his late fifties, has worked with Obinna for eight years. He recognizes Caroline immediately and climbs down. He puts up a smile and immediately proceeds to open the smaller side gate, letting her in.

Still smiling, he holds the gate open. "Madam, E good to see you. Long time, no see."

"E good to see you too, Yang."

"How una dey for house when you comot?" he asks.

"We dey well ooo; how your people dey?"

"We dey fine, except for hunger. Wetin you bring for me?"

Caroline mimics his sad tone of voice. "Nothing ooo, hunger dey everywhere."

"Haba, madam, make you talkan say you no like me na him make you no bring something for me. At all at all, na im worse pass."

"No ooo, how I nogo like you. You na better man. Next time, I no go forget bring something for you."

"Na you talkan, I go remind you," he says. "You na lucky woman, Oga jus dey come back now. He comot say him get early morning meeting."

"Yes ooo, before nko, you no no say me na lucky woman. Thank you."[1]

Caroline walks towards the house, not willing to continue the chat. Her mind is occupied with plans for the future.

The garage door is still open, and Caroline can see her brother helping his steward take out some things from the trunk of his car.

Having heard the gateman open the gate, Obinna looks to see who is coming. To his delight, he sees his sister. He is very much relieved, as

---

1 See back of the book for a translation of this passage of Pidgin English.

he's not ready to deal with any outsider. He's already had a tiresome day with several meetings to attend at his office.

"I'm glad to see you, Nneka," he says. "How have you been?"

Nneka is her native name, and he prefers it to her English name. He gives her a hug.

"I'm fine, Obinna, and I'm glad to see you, too. How are you, Ogochukwu, and the children doing?"

"We are all doing well. What about your husband and children?"

"They are fine and they send their greetings to you."

She is quite encouraged by her brother's joy at seeing her. She no longer entertains any fear about whether he'll be able to help her with money. Her brother has always helped her financially, so why not this time? Perhaps she feels distracted because of the new business venture she's about to get into that her mind is full of concern.

Caroline quickly abandons her fears and makes an effort to concentrate on the present.

"Please come in," Obinna says, leading her into a large sitting room on the main floor.

Her brother has recently changed the furnishings, so Caroline has much to take in. The sitting room has a large bow window and thick, matching leaf-green curtains. The frame of the two-seater sofa is steel with decorative carvings and gold fabric coverings. The two chairs and three-seater sofa feature wooden frames with soft green leather. The air-conditioner is on and soft classical music plays from the stereo.

The décor epitomizes elegance, taste, and class, as easily discerned by a woman of taste. Caroline looks around with keen interest, taking in the scene as she reflects on how her own sitting room back in Lagos used to look. She soaks in the scene and imagines that the sofas are her reverie corner.

But she rouses herself from her daydream, easing herself into the left side of the three-seater with a low groan.

Obinna stands at the stair landing and calls to his wife upstairs. "Ogo, please come. Nneka is here."

"Yes, I'm coming." A moment later, Ogochukwu hurries into the sitting room, smiling.

Ogochukwu does a good job of always looking like a queen in her household. She's a tall, curvy woman with rounded features, and her dimpled smile and gapped teeth enhance her beauty. Today, she's wearing a blouse of finest purple and scarlet lace decked with gold, punctuated around the neckline with red and white diamonds and other precious stones. She's wearing the blouse over a milk-white African George fabric wrapper. The light reflecting off her blouse is blinding, which is why people call her Mirror.

She may be coming back from a meeting, Caroline thinks, assessing her outfit. It's probably worth up to twenty thousand naira.

Caroline meets her in the middle of the room and the two women embrace.

"How are you, my sister?" Caroline asks.

"I am fine, thank God. And what about you?"

"We are well. So what about your children? I haven't seen or heard them."

"Oh, they're on vacation to Kaduna to visit their uncle, Idris. You know, he's now the general manager of Odem Cement."

"I'm happy for him. He's worked hard for the promotion. When are they back?"

"End of next month. We're taking our own vacation by being alone. Please sit down." Ogochukwu motions to the sofa. "Welcome."

Ogochukwu excuses herself to finish supervising the lunch preparation with the steward.

Despite Ogochukwu's show of friendliness, she makes Caroline feel uncomfortable about asking for money. She doesn't also want Ogochukwu to think she, Caroline, isn't worth her salt as a mother, that she isn't able to provide for her children. It's just misfortune; Caroline used to be even more sophisticated and comfortable than her sister-in-law.

As soon as Ogochukwu is out of earshot, Caroline informs her brother why she has come. Fortunately, her brother received last week's message; unfortunately, he is unable to give her the twenty thousand naira. He has only fifteen thousand in the house to spare.

"I will see how I can get the balance to you as soon as possible" he promises. "When is the deadline for the payment?"

"First week of September."

"You did well by looking for the money early. As our people say, it is good to look for the black goat when there's still daylight, because no one will be able to see the black goat in the dark."

Obinna is fond of citing proverbs, unlike his counterparts in the office who no longer value the old traditions. Well, he is often looked upon as wise. Proverbs are not for fools but for the thoughtful.

"We think so, too," Caroline says. "Thank you, my brother. I don't know what I would have done without you."

Just then, Ogochukwu comes in to announce that lunch is ready. The steward helps to set the table and arrange the food and drinks.

Though Ogochukwu didn't catch the conversation, she senses that Caroline must have come to ask for financial help. She's itching to confirm her suspicion.

"You did well to come to see us," Ogochukwu says. "I hope there's no problem?"

Caroline doesn't know how to evade the question, and she doesn't want to lie. She knows Ogochukwu will eventually find out from Obinna why she has come.

She braces herself. "Well there is a little problem. Mathias passed the entrance examination to the Federation Government College. He'll live in a boarding house since the school is very far from Ludu. We need some money so we can register him and pay his tuition and boarding fees. We've managed to save ten thousand naira, but we need twenty thousand more to make it up."

Turning to her husband, Ogochukwu says, "I know Obinna will do something for his sister."

The comment is intended to be complimentary, but it also serves as a mild protest against her husband's generosity. Obinna doesn't always consult her in making such decisions. But what else can she do? She doesn't have any reason to complain, for she has a good job as a schoolteacher and she uses her own earnings however she pleases. Obinna gives her a generous monthly allowance to run the home. He also buys her clothing and expensive gifts from time to time, spoiling her to mark special occasions.

All the same, she would be gratified to help manage her husband's finances, or at least to contribute to decisions. She has often reproached him, claiming that he throws money around and that she doesn't know all the details of his charitable acts. Obinna has always maintained that the money is his and that he has the right to spend it as he likes, provided he takes care of her and their children very well. He also challenges her about how she spends her own money.

Ogochukwu resigns herself to letting the matter rest. She prefers to leave things the way they are rather than push matters too far. She doesn't want to lose her own financial independence.

Obinna catches the mild protest in his wife's comment. "Thank you, Ogo, for being concerned for Nneka, as a good sister in-law would. Fortune, sometimes, becomes an ill wind. It is the responsibility of people who are comfortable to help their relations. I am not the only one comfortable in this house."

Obinna pauses to see if Ogochukwu will share in his pain at seeing his sister's family fall from grace to grass.

"I've never gotten in your way of helping anyone," Ogochukwu retorts. "Whatever you give your sister comes from the two of us. It is not your business alone. Don't speak as though I'm stopping you, as though I don't care about my sister-in-law."

She doesn't want Caroline to think she can always come to them for financial help, but she also doesn't want to be seen as insensitive, hard, and selfish.

"Oh no," Caroline interjects. She hates to be the reason for a quarrel between her brother and his wife. "I must say, the two of you have been good to me."

"That will do now. Please, let's eat," Obinna says.

The three of them enjoy the soup and pounded yam. The egusi soup looks attractive and delicious. It has lots of beef, dried fish, and stockfish. The flavour comes from traditional piper guineense and hot peppers, stimulating the appetite. Bitter leaf has been added to the soup.

Obinna often praises Ogochukwu's cooking. Today he does it deliberately and with emphasis, out of love and in an effort to make up for the open disagreement they had before his sister.

"Ogo, you know the way to your husband's heart," he says. "You have done it again. Thank you."

Ogochukwu responds with a smile. "Thank you."

"My sister, you're more than a teacher," Caroline says. "You can compete with professional chefs. This meal is first grade."

"Thank you, Caroline. I've not forgotten the kind of savoury soup you also cook. You are a better cook than I am."

From the depths of Caroline's heart, she yearns for the years when the quality and flavour of her own soup could measure up to the richness of Ogochukwu's.

"Money answers all things," Caroline says reflectively. "As the common saying goes, *good soup na moni mekam*."[2]

As they eat, they chat about the local news in Ludu.

"When will the village chief, Onwendi, celebrate his ofala?"[3] Obinna asks.

"Next month, August 12," Caroline informs him. "You remember that it usually comes before the New Yam Festival."

Obinna turns to Ogochukwu and changes the subject. "I'm not able to give Nneka the balance of what she needs for Mathias's school fees. I think we may be able to get the money to her if we attend the ofala and the New Yam Festival next month."

"That's fine," Ogochukwu replies. She longs to know how much he has given Caroline already, but that would only make her seem nosy. She resigns herself to making do with what information her husband has given her. Certainly she will be able to find out more later; Obinna is not a secretive person.

---

2 Translation: "It's money that makes soup delicious" or "Delicious soup costs money."

3 An ofala is a big celebration by the traditional ruler. The event is used to commemorate his chieftaincy. It's usually a septennial event; however, some chiefs who are rich may make it a triennial or quadrennial event. It involves huge expenses because of the eating and drinking and entertainment for multitudes of people from all over the country.

CHAPTER NINE

They finish their food and move to the sofa with their drinks and continue the conversation about Ludu. They talk about the new Christian movement that has united the different churches with the common goal of cleansing the community of undesirable forces. Obinna is interested to know more, but Caroline doesn't have enough information; she is neither interested in religion nor in the things of God.

The steward clears the table and Ogochukwu goes to the kitchen to dish out food for the steward, the driver, and the security guard.

Obinna turns to Caroline. "My sister, I'm not probing, but I must tell you that it's not good for your husband to stay home. I think he should return to Lagos to try another business. Look at how life is treating you in the village. You're looking older than your age. Your shop isn't the answer to your family's financial need. I'm not complaining about your husband or whatever help I render to you. Rather, I'm thinking about the future of your family. It's been four years since he lost his business. A healthy life is the greatest treasure, for it is the living who labour, not the dead. One's future is greater than one's past. Onyema can take a loan and begin another business. I can help him get a loan from my bank."

Obinna is the branch manager of First Bank and he's well-respected by his staff and the board of directors. He works very hard and is a guru in the banking industry.

"Thank you for your concern," says Caroline. "You see, Onyema has lost the will to try. We had such an awful experience and I cannot bring myself to tell him to make any further attempts in business until I'm sure we have enough money. You may talk to him yourself, but as for me, I've given up on trying to suggest it, especially now that he's developed the habit of speaking very little and shunning conversation if I ever raise the matter. I had thought he would recover after two or three years, but no, he seems to be pessimistic about everything." Caroline ends with a shrug and a sigh.

Obinna wants to say more, but seeing the pain on her sister's brow, he refrains. Onyema can be stubborn when he chooses to be, and no one can get him to change his mind. Caroline used to be able to convince him, but she seems to have lost that power.

Obinna isn't even sure he wants to talk to his brother-in-law; Onyema might misunderstand him since he's loaning them money for their son's education. He hopes to invite Obinna to Onitsha for a weekend visit so that he can discuss with him the matter of returning to business without appearing insensitive. Knowing how analytical Onyema can be, he wants to think through all the options first.

By the time Ogochukwu comes back into the family room, Caroline looks at the clock behind the sofa.

"I must be leaving so that I'll be able to catch Papa Sunday's bus," she says.

Obinna knows how important it is for her not to miss the bus, so he calls his driver and asks him to take her to the bus terminal. He knows she may want to purchase some supplies first, so she needs to be leaving right away.

Caroline wants to decline the ride, but she knows it would sound strange. She wonders what to do, since she needs to meet up with her new business partner before going back to Ludu. Then it occurs to her that she can instruct the driver where to go without much fuss.

Ogochukwu hands her a bag. "This is for your children."

"Thank you so much," Caroline says as she takes the bag, wondering what might be inside. She takes a peep, but closes the bag quickly since she wants to leave immediately. It's not an acceptable practice to begin to unwrap a present in the presence of the giver.

However, she's impressed. Ogochukwu isn't usually a generous person in terms of gifts.

Obinna is also impressed with his wife, on seeing the bag. He reserves his appreciation for when they are alone together.

As the driver leaves to get the car, Obinna excuses himself. He returns a few minutes later, walks to his sister's side, and hands her a fat brown envelope. She quickly tucks the envelope deep into her handbag. Obinna also hands her a wad of mint naira notes.

"This is for your transport," Obinna says. "And please buy bread for the children on our behalf."

"My brother, you and your wife are just spoiling us. Thank you very much. May the source of all these gifts be replenished to you."

"Amen!" Obinna enthuses.

Obinna instructs the driver to take Caroline to the outskirts of the market so she can buy provisions for her family before boarding the bus.

Caroline embraces her brother and his wife and thanks them again for their hospitality and gifts. She then joins the driver in the front seat.

She waves goodbye, adding, "Till you visit next month, thank you very much for all you've done for us."

"Have a safe trip and greet your family," they respond, waving back.

CHAPTER TEN

As the driver passes the second block up the street, Caroline asks him to turn left. She explains that she wants to check for somebody in a certain restaurant down Bonny Street. The driver obeys.

She asks him to stop in front of a bungalow building. As she opens the door to get out, she says, "Please wait for me in the car. I won't be long. I'm supposed to travel back with my friend, and this is our agreed meeting spot. I'll only be a minute, unless I have to look around for her."

As soon as Caroline walks into the restaurant, she meets the girl who served the drinks earlier. The girl asks her to sit down while she goes to call Mr. Unna, who appears immediately.

"Madam, you're back," he says. "All right, are you ready to make your deposit? By next week I shall bring twenty pieces of Hollandaise wrapper to you, as the first consignment."

"Yes. How much must I deposit today?"

"I can allow you to have the first consignment if you deposit twenty thousand naira," Unna responds in his usual business-like tone.

Caroline's heart jumps. She doesn't have that amount of money on her, and even if she had it, how could she part with her son's school fees just like that? She is quiet and Unna is forced to look her right in the eyes.

He notices that her cheerful countenance has turned into a frown. "Madam, what is the problem? You are not a novice in business, for you know how much Hollandaise Wax costs apiece. One may cost up to six thousand naira, depending on the design. Have you forgotten that you can make a profit by selling above the minimum price? When I saw you this morning, I knew you were the right person for this contract. I believe I was not wrong about my perception of you."

Caroline still doesn't answer, for she's thinking about how to explain to her husband that she has "invested" all the money she got from her brother in hopes of a quick profit. She can almost feel how devastating it would be if this venture fails. She fears for her family, especially her husband, who's already in low spirits.

She looks straight into Unna's eyes. "Sorry, I cannot do this," she says, with all the firmness she can muster. "I don't have the money. What I have is my son's school fees, and it's not the amount you're asking. Let's leave this for now; I may have money someday, and I will do the business with you then."

"All right. How much are you able to deposit? I'm asking because I really want to help you."

"If you will accept two thousand naira as the first installment, we can do business."

Mr. Unna is silent, surprised at her sudden resolve to not do business unless he accepts.

"Well, if you're not interested in the business, you'll be the one to regret it, not me. I've tried to help you—"

Just then, the waitress approaches their table to find out if they want something to drink. She cuts Mr. Unna short and addresses Caroline: "How strange it is that some people find it difficult to recognize a good business opportunity when they see it!" she exclaims. "My name is Nancy. My sister, I was like you when I first met Mr. Unna. I never believed him, even though I heard stories about how he has helped people make money. Let me tell you, seeing is believing! You've seen me now; therefore believe, and don't throw away your luck. I have benefited greatly from this business. You are very lucky. I work in this restaurant, but I have a huge wholesale business. Retailers buy off my materials as soon as they arrive. I've already sold out my consignment for the next two weeks. I asked Mr. Unna to supply more clothes next week, but he said that the next consignment is for another person. I guess you're the person he referred to, and you want to throw away your luck?" She pauses, looking at Caroline's face searchingly. "It was not by accident that I came around your table just now and overheard your conversation. It was ordained so that I can tell you my story."

Unna is grateful for the girl's convincing testimony. These are the proofs Caroline needs to make the hoped for good decision.

"Thank you, Nancy, for being so kind to let Mrs. Okwueze know the truth about this business," Unna says. "We often need to see the truth from another's perspective in order to be convinced."

"It's my pleasure," Nancy responds.

Unna continues in the same spirit of irrefutable evidence. "Look, madam, I have helped people like you to become rich. I appreciate your excuse, but the best your excuse can do is rob you of your rightful good fortune. You see, sometimes we rob ourselves of what should rightly belong to us, supposing that other people are robbing us. I just want to help you; therefore, I will reduce the deposit to sixteen thousand naira. I'm doing this to show you my strong support in helping your family rebuild the business you lost to fraudsters."

Caroline's initial conviction about the genuineness of the offer rises again. She knows that all investments come with risks.

"That will not do," she says. "I was able to get fifteen thousand naira from my brother."

"Ok, I can manage that, just because it is you. Ask Nancy. She is my witness that I usually don't hit my rock-bottom price in this manner. Deposit the fifteen thousand naira today and I will bring the twenty pieces of Hollandaise Wax wrapper to you early next week. I have never been this cheap. You are a lucky businesswoman."

Without any second thought or premonition, Caroline reaches into her handbag and draws out the brown envelope. She counts the money and gives it to Unna, who in turn takes it and gives the wad of mint naira notes to Nancy, who proceeds to count them.

"I want Nancy to be the witness," Unna says. "She'll help to count the money, but I'm not so much interested in this deposit as I am in helping you. You behaved like a wise woman." He rubs his palms together like a diviner waiting for a response from the oracle to whom he has presented an offering

Nancy counts the money meticulously, and then announces that the money is exactly fifteen thousand naira. She hands the wad of crisp notes to Unna. He takes the bundle and turns to Caroline.

"Your husband will be proud of you for making this wise move. Please tell him that Mr. Aubrey Unna greets him. I will bring the wrappers to you by Wednesday next week. I know your village, and I can locate your house from the market square by following the footpath by the apple trees on the left. Your house is not very far from the square."

Caroline is impressed and becomes even more convinced about the validity of the business.

Mr. Unna must be an angel sent to help me, she concludes. "Yes, we live a bit close to the market square, as soon as you turn off the major road by the barber's shop along the footpath lined by apple trees on the left."

"I know you, as I have said before. You have seen my office and you have also met Nancy, who is one of my business agents and our witness in today's transaction. You still remember that I am from Mbia. Don't forget that. I will see you in a few days' time, madam."

"What about my receipt for the deposit?"

"Oh sorry, I forgot. I'll get that to you presently. Just a second here." He goes into his office and comes back with a receipt booklet. He proceeds to complete it, then tears it out and gives it to Caroline. "Of course, you know that this piece of paper is nothing when you compare it to our mutual agreement. I look forward to reconnecting with the wife of my one-time business acquaintance."

"Thank you very much, Mr. Unna."

"It's my pleasure to partner with you. Don't forget to wish your husband well."

"Have a safe trip," Nancy says.

Caroline leaves the restaurant, feeling content about the feat she has accomplished. She is looking forward to the years of prosperity ahead, and being heralded by her husband.

CHAPTER ELEVEN

By the time she returns to the car, the driver is very worried, but he has sat patiently, waiting and wondering.

"Madam, what about your friend?" he asks.

Caroline has nearly forgotten her pretext, having been preoccupied with the riches that will soon be hers. She quickly recollects herself. "I don't know. I couldn't find her. Please hurry to the bus terminal so I don't miss the bus. I'm not able to buy anything for my children just now. I'll get something from hawkers on the highway, or from a supermarket if Papa Sunday stops to buy fuel."

They get to the terminal and Caroline bids the driver goodbye. Almost all of the passengers are already seated and Papa Sunday is checking to make sure the luggage is tightly secured. Caroline has made it just in time.

The journey back to Ludu goes well. Most of the passengers chat about the business that took them to Onitsha. Caroline doesn't have much to share. She complains only about the heavy traffic and how badly she needs to get home.

She arrives home safely, but as soon as she steps into her house she feels something give way in her. She experiences a sickening feeling in the pit of her stomach, followed by a sudden swing in her emotion. Immediately she feels a premonition that she must have done a foolish thing by giving that man the fifteen thousand naira she got from her brother. She chides herself for entertaining such thoughts. She must remain positive and calm, and endeavour not to discuss anything until the following Wednesday.

She gives her children the gifts Ogochukwu sent. She is impressed to find that Ogochukwu bought clothes for all the children.

Caroline doesn't tell her husband much about the trip. She simply informs him that the trip went well and that her brother gave her some money and that he will bring the balance next week. Onyema wants to know how much she was able to get; he finds it strange that she doesn't tell him the amount immediately. But he has been withdrawn for a long time, so he judges it right to give his wife room to be withdrawn, too, if she needs to. This works out well for Caroline, since she would have been unable to handle such a discussion in her present state of mind.

Chapter Twelve

By Thursday night, Caroline is convinced that Unna will not honour the contract. She waits until Friday night to tell her husband the details about her trip to Onitsha. She can no longer postpone the story, because she knows her brother will visit the next week during the ofala festival and will bring her the five thousand naira balance for her son's school fees.

Onyema listens through her story. He is speechless with shock that his wife would part with such a lump sum of money without any tangible commitment on the part of the so-called businessman, except a fake receipt and a verbal promise that is vain at best. He is surprised that his wife, who used to be so shrewd, has fallen to such gullibility—his wife, who understands the subtleties of business and uses every faculty and natural endowment of insight to analyze and determine the validity and profitability of any business investment and is mostly accurate… It is incomprehensible that she would fall into this kind of error. It is a very hard pill to swallow, and it may have grave repercussions on their future decisions.

Caroline had hoped her husband knew the man so they could find a way of getting back the money from him. To her dismay, her husband does not know Mr. Unna in any way. Her fear has come true and all her hopes and confidence are blown away like chaff in the face of a storm of lies and greed. She feels very cold, lonely, and lost. Where can she turn? She has disappointed her brother and betrayed her family. She manages to convince her husband not to tell Obinna what she did with the money.

Two weeks after the incident, Mr. Unna still hasn't come or sent any word. Obinna brought them the balance, as promised, and Caroline spent the night after her brother's visit in bitterness and regret.

She lies tossing and turning all through the night. Her mind is in turmoil and her heart heavy. One thing she hopes to do is trace the restaurant to see if she can find Mr. Unna or Nancy. However, she is unable to return to Onitsha without incurring more expenses and exposing herself to further heartaches.

For years, Caroline has been the family's financial manager and treasurer. Now Onyema asks her to surrender to him all the money in her possession. Caroline is only too glad to do it, if it will appease Onyema and perhaps help to reverse her costly error in judgement.

As soon as there's enough light to walk outside, she runs to Mama Joe's house.

Since the change Mama Joe underwent, she has become more interested in mentoring young women. Caroline has been observing the change with interest and hoping for an opportunity to relate more personally with Mama Joe. She decides that this financial challenge is an opportunity to establish a closer relationship with Mama.

Mama listens patiently as Caroline tells her everything about their financial crunch, especially their desperation to pay their son's school fees. She wants to know if there's support, in any way, Mama Joe could render to her.

"I don't know what I can do for you," Mama says. "But I am glad that you decided to share your problem with me."

"Thank you, Mama. I know your hands are full. It would be very selfish of me to think of asking you for a loan. I am here only to ask for your advice."

"I don't know what to advise on this matter. I may be able to offer a little financial help from the money I've been saving for Joe's university education. Nevertheless, I can't promise anything definitely. Please take care of yourself. Problems come and go, but don't allow problems to swallow you up." Mama observes her for a while and then adds, "I have been meaning to discuss something with you."

Caroline looks up meekly and expectantly.

"I wanted to ask why you and Onyema are not members of the church," Mama continues. "Have you ever considered joining a church?"

Caroline hasn't expected to talk about religion with Mama. Because Mama is an elderly woman and may be her benefactress, she is compelled to respond.

"I don't know, Mama. I guess we don't find any need for it. Joining a church, or worshipping anything or anyone, hasn't been a concern for our family. We don't hurt anyone or need anything from any god."

She chooses her words carefully, because Mama is a respectable and experienced woman in all circles—agnostics and believers, rich and poor. Mama has become very devoted to God and is well esteemed in town—and even beyond—for being economically well off. She is revered for her industry and generosity.

That is the respect you gain by being affluent and generous, Caroline thinks. *Doesn't a rich woman retain honour? Doesn't one's gifts earn one respect and position in society?*

Caroline looks at Mama Joe with admiration. She doesn't dismiss Mama's question about joining the church as lightly as she would have if the suggestion had come from someone less prominent.

"Well, I want you to think about joining a church," Mama says. "I can visit you and Onyema tomorrow to talk about it. You're young and you need such a relationship to provide an anchor for the future."

Because Caroline is at her lowest ebb, she doesn't resist Mama's suggestion. She feels a little bit better for having talked to someone who listens without condemning her.

The next day, Mama visits them and proposes that Caroline join her business as an apprentice. Both Caroline and Onyema warm up to the idea. Promptly, they agree that Caroline may start work at Mama's confectionery the next week.

Then Mama invites both of them to church. Onyema bluntly refuses to make any commitment. He politely requests that Mama not mention it again.

"Even if I have become poor, I am not superstitious," he says to Mama.

"This is not superstition," Mama says. "It is about life. It's about having a relationship with God as your father through Jesus as your saviour."

"That will do. I don't discuss such things with anybody. You have done well by inviting Caroline to become your apprentice. You may talk to her about religion. She may need it, since she has become a dupe. She can take the children so they, too, will have an opportunity to decide for themselves if they need religion or not. As for me, I don't need religion."

Caroline looks at her husband with a frown, but his indictment has lost its power to make her ashamed.

Chapter Thirteen

From working with Mama, Caroline starts taking her children with her to church. Onyema is not bothered. He enjoys the quietness in the house when they're all gone. He entertains himself by drinking beer and reading old newspapers and magazines. Mama loans them money with which to pay their son's school fees.

As the weeks turn to months, Onyema watches with interest the changes that gradually come upon his wife. She no longer painstakingly calculates the cost of everything each night and looking distraught. She looks more cheerful and has a more optimistic outlook than before.

Caroline begins to earn some contracts through Mama's help. She works hard at the business and learns very fast. Before long, their finances improve and they have fewer worries about money. Caroline is also more content and seldom complains about money. Onyema even thinks she looks more attractive. He notices how smooth her skin is. The lines he used to notice around her eyes and forehead are very faint. Caroline is a slim ebony woman, her pear-shaped body enhancing her features.

Onyema begins to pay more attention to her appearance and appreciates afresh her beauty. He feels a tinge of jealousy that she goes to church without him and that other men might be attracted to her. He brushes this off by assuring himself that she is his alone. However, he looks for convenient opportunities to hold her in his arms and show her affection as in the days of their courtship.

One Sunday, as Caroline is getting ready for church, Onyema asks to know when she will be back. She's surprised at the question and wants to know why he would ask, but she judges it better not to say anything. She wants the peace and freedom to continue going to church.

"I will be back around 11.00 a.m.," she responds.

"All right. That will be fine," he says without further comment.

Caroline expects him to say more, but he does not. She turns to look at him and finds him watching her keenly. Their eyes meet, then they quickly look away. She concludes that he must be lonely in the house on Sundays, longing for her companionship. She brushes the thought aside.

Well, Onyema has never lacked friends, she thinks. *He can visit his friends to keep him company while I go to church.*

However, deep inside she is curious to know why he has asked the question. He never seemed to care about how long she stayed at church before as long as she comes home eventually.

Caroline and the children come home and find Onyema in the kitchen making lunch. It's been a long time since he last cooked for the family. He learned to cook when growing up; he had no sisters, so his mother made all her five boys learn how to cook. Today he is making stew and rice with beef. She helps him to finish the lunch.

Rather than leave the house right after lunch as he used to do, he stays around. He even invites her for a siesta that afternoon. Onyema is softening in his attitude, becoming more communicative. He helps Caroline by working with her when she's decorating cakes. Their love and respect for one another grows anew.

Caroline appreciates the fact that she decided to start attending church. The benefits make an impact on her, but the ripple effect on her husband is even more profound. Whatever is affecting her is rubbing off on Onyema. The quality of their communication and intimacy is increasing.

CHAPTER FOURTEEN

One year later, on an early Monday morning, Caroline leaves for Mama's house earlier than usual.

"How are you, Caroline?" Mama asks, more concerned about Caroline's looks than the early hour. "You look tired. Did you sleep well last night?"

"I'm fine, but no, I didn't sleep well."

"Why are you so early then?"

"I have something to discuss with you," Caroline begins. "Last night I had a dream. I saw a woman whom I have often seen in my dreams. The woman most likely possesses supernatural powers. She often tells me things, and most times what she tells me comes to pass. She told me that my husband's business would fail and that something very serious would happen to me in the month of July last year. The fact is that all her predictions came true. Last night, I saw the woman again, and she told me to stop working with you and to be careful not to participate in the town-wide Christian program to which you have invited me. She said that if I attend the program, I might not survive childbirth in the future. You remember that Onyema and I really want to have a fourth child, to see if we'll get a baby girl. Mama, I don't know what to do."

Mama smiles. She doesn't respond immediately, but she looks at Caroline with keen interest. "Since you started working with me, have you gained or lost?"

"I have gained, Mama," Caroline answers meekly.

"Since you started going to church, did your life become better or worse? Have you lost anything from associating with the people at the church?"

"I have not lost anything."

"Now decide for yourself what you should do. You may decide to listen to the voice that guides you and has been able to predict everything that has come true in your life. You may also decide to ignore the voice and follow your judgement. Did you tell your husband, hoping that he would exercise his talent for anti-superstition? Don't forget that exercising faith is different from being superstitious."

"I told him, but of course Onyema doesn't believe in anything. He doesn't believe in God or in Ogwugwu or even in any voice or spirit. He said that I was only imagining things. He said that the woman's voice was my imagination and that even though it has predicted things that have happened, it may still be the voice of my intuition. He said that I should ignore it and do what I think is best for me."

"Onyema may not be entirely correct, but he has made a point," Mama says. "All I want to encourage you to do is to make an effort to attend the August program. Again, you need to confront this woman and refuse her predictions. Free yourself from her control. My daughter, this is your life and the choice is yours. Don't let anybody, whether human or spirit, run your life for you. You pay for what you want and live with what you get. Remember that nothing is written in stone. You can change anything if you rise to the challenge."

Caroline feels exasperated. "You're saying the same thing as Onyema."

"Yes, that's right. So what will you decide?"

"I think I want to take the woman's advice. I hope you'll not be offended, since you have helped me by teaching me your business without charging me anything." She faces Mama with a mixture of firmness and meekness.

"Okay, Caroline," Mama says with motherly love and concern. "I want to remind you that you were created with the powerful tool of choice. What you choose or allow will rule you. I must warn you, however: having already bought into this spirit woman's trade, you may have to fight hard to be free from her control. Nevertheless, if you fight her today, painful though it may be, you will see tomorrow that the fight was worth it."

Caroline is surprised that Mama should suggest that she resist the voice. After all, the voice has revealed things to her since she was sixteen years of age. She has known that voice and has cherished the relationship.

I'm not sure why I should resist her, Caroline thinks, rationalizing her decision. *I can do the business on my own. As for the program, it's only a program. It's not the end of the world.*

"Thank you, Mama," she says as she gets up to leave. "It's always good to talk with you."

"My dear, I still want you to think about your decision. The choices we make today affect us tomorrow. There are lasting impacts for generations to come, unless something more powerful rises to challenge their impact." Mama walks her to the small gate. "I expect you to continue working with me until you're fully established."

Throughout the day, however, Caroline doesn't show up for work.

The next day, Caroline sends her son to tell Mama that she will not be back to work for at least two weeks. She doesn't offer any explanation.

Mama isn't disturbed, but she determines in her heart that before Caroline is allowed to work for her again, they must redefine the terms of their contract. They only had a verbal agreement at the beginning, and Mama has charged nothing.

Mama is puzzled as to why Caroline is so convinced that the spirit woman is working for her benefit. If that were so, why would the spirit woman specifically tell her to stop working with Mama?

She is upset because she took Caroline in when she was desperate. She helped her, taught her a trade, and allowed her to manage some contracts for her own financial benefit, not Mama's. She marvels at the spirit woman's deception. Just when things are beginning to look bright for Caroline, this woman comes around to spoil the game.

Mama feels very sad at Caroline's ignorant about being taken advantage of through supernatural manipulation. She decides to wait until Caroline comes around again. In the meantime, she will pray for Caroline and not be angry with her.

CHAPTER FIFTEEN

Mama's business continues to thrive. Even though she takes on apprentices from time to time, her children are her most committed workers, and they are very enterprising. They are eager to assist her and are appreciative of her as their mother. In fact, her household has become a hive of industry. She is very proud of them and considers them as arrows in the hand of the mighty.

When people owe her money, she sometimes forgives the debt, when she can afford to do so, especially and if they have a good attitude. Even though she's generous, however, she doesn't easily succumb to intimidation from debtors.

A man named Mr. Buford Ozem owes her money and has refused to pay for over a year. Mama made a ten-tier wedding cake for Buford's wedding. She also supplied all the drinks, desserts, and main course. Buford's wedding was the talk of the town because of the lavish reception, especially the quality of the food, yet Buford refused to pay, claiming that his business wasn't doing well.

Mama gave him a year to come up with the money. She was generous, but Buford failed to make serious plans to pay the debt. She approached Buford several times to ask for the balance. Initially, he was very apologetic and made promises and set deadlines for payment. He broke every one of his promises.

One full year later, Mama's patience has run out. Without recourse, she goes to him one morning and firmly demands that the balance be paid immediately. Buford's reaction is to tell her that he expected understanding from her, because he is starting a new family. His wife, pregnant with their first child, has just finished her teacher's training and is not yet working. He also needs to finish building their house.

"What do you still need money for?" he asks. "Your husband has built you a house and set up a business for you. I don't understand why you are impatient about the money. I have said that I will pay you the money. What else do you want me to do?"

Mama is shocked at Buford's reaction, because she thought he had more sense than to say such things. She has gone out of her way to help him during his wedding in order to encourage him, as she often does for young families.

Mama observes him for a while without saying anything. Then, calmly and firmly, she says, "Buford, this is the last time I'll talk to you about this money, but make no mistake: you must pay the whole amount, to the last kobo."

"Will you force me?" he asks. "You don't need the money, and you do not understand that I've been making an effort to pay you. Therefore, regard the matter as closed. Let matters rest."

Her face showing no expression, Mama simply walks away without responding.

Buford expected her to argue further with him. Her silence has made him uncomfortable. A saying comes to his mind about being cautious when somebody you have wronged keeps silent. A cautionary tale is told of a mother kite who sends her young ones to capture chickens from a mother hen. They go to the first hen and take a couple of her chicks. The mother hen runs around, screaming, flapping her wings, flying up and down, and making a resounding noise. When the chicks are brought to the mother kite, she asks her young kite messengers what the mother hen did.

"She just flew around, flapped her wings, ran up and down, and made a lot of noise," the young ones say.

"Was that all?" she asks them.

"Yes, that was all."

"Then we're going to eat the chicks, for their mother couldn't do much beyond making noise and flapping her wings."

They eat the chicks.

The mother kite then sends them out again. They find another mother hen with chicks. They swoop down and carry off a couple of the chicks. The mother hen completely ignores them and continues to feed her remaining chicks.

When the young kite messenger returns to their mother, she asks them, "What did the mother hen do when you carried away her chicks?"

"She cast a glance at us, then ignored us and continued to feed her remaining chicks."

"Okay. We are not going to eat these chicks. Take them back, because when you have wronged someone and the person doesn't say anything, you must beware; you don't know what he or she has in mind. She is confident and may retaliate in a manner that is unprecedented."

———

Mama goes away very disappointed and grieved, but she resolves that Buford must pay the money by whatever means possible. Mama had hoped to use the money to pay for Nwakaego's third year of tuition at the nursing school.

That evening, she calls all her children and recounts the incident to them.

"I'm still thinking about how to make him pay," she says.

Joe takes Buford's effrontery personal and considers himself the aggrieved party. He's convinced that Buford's is trying to take advantage of his mother's generosity.

"Mama, don't worry," Joe says calmly. "I promise to get that money for you before next month ends."

Mama is surprised to hear Joe talk in this way, but she has learned to respect the determination with which Joe tackles challenges.

Joe visits Buford one evening, a week later, just as Buford is about to shut down his carpentry shop for the day. All of his apprentices have left for home.

Joe, in a blue t-shirt and khaki trousers and wearing thick sunglasses, greets him and says that he has something very important to tell him.

"Okay," Buford says. "So long as it's a very short message. I need to go home."

"No problem. It's not going to take long." Joe clears his throat. "You know my father died when I was only six years old. We were able to survive and to become what we are today because of hard work. Ten years is a long time for a boy who lost his father at an early age to grow up and assume the responsibility of being the man of the house."

Buford is surprised, for he never reckoned that a youth of sixteen years could talk to a man of thirty-five years in this way while looking him full in the face.

It's disrespectful enough to look elders in the eye when talking to them, he thinks, sighing under his breath, *but with what word can one describe a youth who not only looks an elder in the eye but also claims to be his equal? Things have changed.*

Joe guesses what Buford is thinking. "Just as you are the man of your house, so am I the man in my father's household. I work very hard and I cannot live there and see you insult my mother as though she is a poor widow without an heir."

"Things are awry in this land," Buford says, shaking his head. "What an abomination that small children these days no longer know their elders. Young man, I advise you to go home. I have no matter to settle with you. I'll talk to your mother later."

"I did respect you, Mr. Ozem, and that is why I held my peace all the while, expecting you to pay what you owed. It is said that if a chicken runs too much, you give it a hot pursuit. You have taken too much, and from a woman who has done so much good for you and sacrificed to give you the best wedding reception there ever was around here. I want you to know that the money you owe my mother is due by the end of this month."

"Young man, don't provoke me! Enough of this insult," Buford thunders in palpable anger. "How dare you speak to me in proverbs? When a young boy isn't old enough to wear the loincloth but chooses to wear it prematurely, the wind will carry both away."

Joe is unruffled. "Anybody who knows how to hold his own can use proverbs, whether young or old. Mr. Ozem, certainly we are now speaking like men. I respect you as a man. You will also respect me as a man, regardless of my age. I am responsible for my father's family and I will not let you insult my mother. When a father sends his child on an errand, the child goes with boldness. The spirit of responsibility, in response to the pride I have in my father, urges me to defend the family he left behind. My legitimate and simple demand is that you pay what you owe." He pauses, then gets up to leave "I thank you for granting this audience. We will soon know who's wearing the loincloth prematurely."

Buford is up to his neck with hatred and disdain for this youth, yet he is incapable of doing anything because of the incredible effect of his words, composure, and courage. He figures that it may be because of Joe that Mama chose not to argue with him.

He also notes that physically he's no match for Joe. Joe is six feet tall and heavily built. Nonetheless, he makes an attempt to exhibit authority.

"Young man," Buford says with intimidation, "since you no longer know your elder and have come to insult me, I'll tell you right here that I will never pay that money. I've had enough of your insults."

Joe stops at the door to the shop and leans lightly on the handle. "Mr. Ozem, you may never have told any lie in your life, but you can count what you have just said as the first lie."

He walks away, leaving Buford in deep dismay. Dazed, he tries to imagine what has come upon the youth of these days that they would meddle in the affairs of their elders. Buford is convinced that Joe is high on weed, or maybe even drunk. What else could explain Joe's behaviour?

Joe plans to cart away Buford's toolbox if he fails to pay the money. Then he will go to the site of his new house and confiscate important tools and materials. Finally, he'll report him to the council of elders for oppressing his mother. He will call up witnesses against him.

That boy's boldness is unnerving, Buford thinks once Joe has left. *The way he used proverbs and talked with such composure, as a man who knew exactly what he was doing... it demonstrates that I might have to fight hard against his threats. I may not succeed, for he may have people behind him.*

"The elders say that when you wake in the morning and your chicken begins to chase you, you have to run because you cannot tell whether the chicken has developed fangs in the night," he says to himself. "The elders also say that a chicken doesn't dance on the road for nothing if there is no hidden emissary beating the drums nearby."

That night, Buford lies on his bed, thinking about the whole matter and trying to make up his mind about what to do.

———

Buford pays half of the balance before the end of the month. He pleads with Mama to allow him to pay the rest in two months' time. Mama wisely tells him that the matter is out of her hand and that he is dealing with Joe.

Later, Joe sends a message, informing him that the money must be paid the following week. If not, he won't know what to tell his friends and the council of elders, who has heard about the matter and are waiting to see if Buford pays.

At that, Buford understands that the matter is more serious than he imagined. Many of the council members will not support him if they know how long he has owed Mama. Mama is known as a generous woman who has helped many people, so he will have no one to support him.

Buford had hoped to intimidate her and bury the matter between them, paying nothing more than his initial deposit. After all, was he not building a house and Mama already had a house?

He pays up everything, but he nurses a grudge against Joe.

CHAPTER SIXTEEN

The committee set up by the Christian Association of Ludu is finally able to bring over the Christian group from Lagos. It's not easy, since the group is booked solid most weekends of the year. The meeting is scheduled for three days (Thursday to Saturday) in August 1992. The group arrives on Wednesday evening with their musical gadgets, various Christian literature on all manner of subjects, audiotapes for music, and numerous teaching resources. They come with traditional and modern musical instruments of both African and Western origins. Their African musical instruments include shakers, kalimbas, udus, African bells, xylophones, and drums such as djembes and doumbeks. For their Western instruments, they have drum kits, different types of guitars, tympanis, trumpets, violas, trombones, tubas, clarinets, tambourines, violins, and cymbals. These intercontinental musicians are ready to shake Ludu with their wide palette of sound.

As early as 1:00 p.m. on Thursday, they begin to set up. The village arena comes alive with people gathering to check out what's going on. By evening, gospel music is heard far and wide. The ensemble sings with all its might. People come out of curiosity. People come to gossip. People come to meet their neighbours. People come for their needs to be met. People come as though the throb of music resonates with their heartbeats. They understand and respond to the language of music.

The month of August is suitable for such a program because it's the time of the harvest time and people have less work to do on their farms. Also, people who live in the cities use the time to visit towns and villages to participate in these kinds of events.

The program is set to begin at 4:00 p.m. The music blasts from mounted sound systems and many people sway to the music. The people here don't care what kind of music they dance to so long as it touches the soul. Music provides a point of identification for them. The people love music, whether in praise of Ogwugwu or Almighty God. "God" is a common word in most households. Religion is the breath and food of the community. When somebody dies or when there is a celebration, the people mark the event with music. Improvisation in music and dance happens all the time.

By the time Mama Joe arrives, the town square is half filled, even though she's an hour early. She is thankful to find a spot to set down her bench. She sits with her four children.

Joe has been helping the visitors mount their musical instruments and has been running errands to assist them. People aren't surprised to see him actively helping the visitors. He is good at running errands and has been playing a very important part in the family business, especially with getting supplies for the bakery, since he is the only one who can drive their pick-up van.

He has always lived in Ludu, but soon Joe will visit Lagos, where his uncle from his mother's side has invited him to spend a month at his company, to expose him to life outside Ludu. After all, one day Joe will have to leave the town to attend university.

Until recently, Mama was concerned that Joe had gone too far with his Christian faith. He energetically supports any course that he believes will help people to see the light of Jesus. However, since her own conversion after the incident at the stream, she is no longer worried.

Two years ago, she became a member of the Scripture Union and began to attend their Monday meetings. She once considered people who attended such meetings to be indolent and passive, wasting their time with meetings and prayers. In the town, these people are generally disdained and disparagingly called ndinkuaka—the "clapping people." The first members were mostly youths and children. Then some women and a few men joined, but none of the rich or influential people.

Mr. Augustine Ojia became the first person of economic impact to join the group. He runs a thriving supermarket and drugstore. Before he became a member, he allowed the group to rent a large upper room in his two-storey building. When people asked him why he did that, he was initially defensive. Later he made it clear that it was nobody's business. People then weren't surprised when he and his family join the Scripture Union.

Mama Joe was the second person of influence to join. People concluded that she joined because of her son. However, when they began to see the changes in her, they were convinced that something must have happened—but nobody asked her what it was.

CHAPTER SEVENTEEN

Mama is unable to focus her thoughts for a long time, distracted by the sight of Joe running around and helping the visitors get started. He seems to be in many places at once. She reflects on the time, two years ago, when she wouldn't have had anything to do with these people. She had considered them to be nothing more than Jesus fanatics.

Life has many surprised, she muses. *No condition, whether spiritual or physical, is permanent.*

Soon the arena is filled with people standing or sitting wherever they are able to find space. Some children even climb trees in order to watch what's happening on stage. The music is booming and people dance, clap, and jump. Some people are busy catching up with neighbours; others stand aloof, watching without any obvious interest.

The preacher, a chocolate-complexioned man of average height in his early thirties, mounts the podium at exactly 5:30 p.m. He wears a three-piece suit and his short brown hair is well-groomed. Without anyone introducing him, he starts off the meeting and announces himself as Brother Goodnews. He's a handsome and confident man with dignified features.

He takes a long time introducing himself, especially his background. He is from Oka and didn't know his father or have any father figure in his life. His mother, the priestess of Ocharaoma, was free to take in any lovers she fancied. The man who fathered her son didn't have any claim on him, so it wasn't important for him to know his biological father.

Brother Goodnews says that he was destined to be a great traditional medicine man because his mother taught him the secret language of leaves in the forest and the medicinal properties of different herbs. He began to explore his skills in this trade by elementary school. He prepared concoctions and sold them to vendors who recognized his power as the son of the priestess. Most times, people testified to getting better by using his concoctions. They showered him with gifts and honour.

He was a brilliant student. By the age of sixteen, he finished high school and went to university in Ile-Ife to study chemical engineering. His mother was responsible for paying his tuition, but he was responsible for all other expenses. Yet he was a rich student and had more than he needed.

"I am a child of destiny," he announces. "The circumstances of my birth shape who I am today. God is always a winner, for all powers belong to Him. Well, I ran my life my own way. I was a confident young man who always looked out for fun. I had a group of friends who I ran around with on campus. I thought it a lot of fun to spy on students who called themselves Christians. I was curious to know what they did in their meetings.

"One Sunday afternoon, I secretly attended a meeting of a Christian group on campus. To my surprise, I found some good-looking girls who also came from wealthy families. They were gorgeously dressed. I used to think most Bible-carrying girls were dull, disagreeable, and poor. I wanted to get one of these girls to join my chain of girlfriends, because I'd heard that Christians shunned such relationships. My heart began to scheme about how to do it. I had money, influence, attraction, and I knew some secrets about spiritualism. I decided to get one of these girls pregnant, to show these so-called Christians were spurious.

"Instead I had an unexpected encounter with Jesus during one of their meetings. I passed through many difficulties and challenges because of my new lifestyle, but I didn't give up and God preserved my life, delivered me, and gave me the power to overcome temptations. Today, I have come to this village to proclaim the deliverance and power of God to all who will dare to believe. I am much better off as a Christian than I was before."

His confidence is contagious, and he holds their attention right to the end of his story. The text of his sermon is from Mark 11:22–24. He speaks as though he has all the powers of heaven and earth at his service.

While his story is compelling, some conclude that he may be insane. Others conclude that he is a boastful and arrogant fellow not worth being taken seriously. Nevertheless, others believe. It is undeniable that he's a handsome and intelligent young man, full of charisma with having a good sense of humour. Hence, they keep listening.

His voice echoes with authority. "I say, folks, with faith you can say to this mountain, be ye removed and be cast into the midst of the sea, and if you have no doubt you shall have what you say. When you say yes to God's open arms, the foundation of salvation will be laid on your life. When you say yes to Jesus, He will say yes to you. Jesus Christ overcame the devil and his cohorts and you are to reign in life with Him because He already purchased victory for you. The apostles demonstrated the same power over the kingdom of darkness. You can do it, too."

He gives many instances in his life when he faced obstacles, even death, but was victorious through faith. His success stories are replete with challenges, with no failures. He claims that his faith helps him through.

However, his audience is not yet sure how faith works.

Joe listens with both his ears and mouth open. He doesn't want to miss even the least detail. He is thirsty for action, and this is his chance. He is familiar with the text of the sermon, and he has always been intrigued by how a simple declaration of faith can have such an impact on grim situations.

Joe is determined to see that every mountain moves, especially Ogwugwu, whose shrine is set at the foot of the hills. The shrine is well kept, for he is the most famous deity in the town. Ogwugwu is reputed to have defended the people during the tribal wars. It is even said that he prevented the Nigerian soldiers from entering the town of Ludu during the civil war of 1967–1970. The townspeople and their neighbouring towns fear Ogwugwu. People as far as Agaru come to worship him during the Ogwugwu festival.

The preacher ends his sermon and calls for people who need prayer. He first prays for those who want to have a born-again experience. He leads them in the following prayer: "Lord Jesus, I acknowledge that You died for my sins. I repent of my sins. Please come into my life. I make

You my Saviour and Lord from this day forward. I thank You for answering my prayers. Amen."

He then prays for those who need healing and deliverance. Finally, he offers a prayer of blessing upon everyone. The meeting ends at about 8:00 p.m.

CHAPTER EIGHTEEN

The next afternoon's meeting continues in the same manner. Goodnews preaches on faith and the power of the Holy Spirit. In closing, he prays for more people who need healing. He then prays with people who respond to his invitation to be empowered.

"This is the night of defining territories," he says. "You are empowered to wage war against all the forces of demons. You will come back with testimonies, because nothing will hurt you. This town ought to have progressed beyond this level. We ought to see many rich people come from this town. People's lives have stagnated and been impoverished because of the many gods they worshipped and to whom they made endless sacrifices. The people are caged and need to be liberated today in the name of Jesus. All of you standing in front of this stage are empowered to demolish shrines and charms both in your homes and in the town. Set the people free. Set them at liberty from everything that holds them back and limits the full expression of their God-given potential. Now is the time, for tomorrow may be too late. Go and set the captives free and bring Jesus's abundant life to the people. Go, go, go, go..."

His voice rings. The faithful begin to spread out like smoke that has been trapped in a furnace, released suddenly in the face of a gentle wind.

The people are to cleanse the land by destroying idols, charms, and images that represent demonic forces wherever they are found. They are to reassemble at the school hall by 7:30 p.m. to share their testimonies and participate in a prayer meeting in preparation for the last night of the meeting, where they shall see a greater demonstration of power.

Some people lose interest in him, convinced that he is out of his mind. Some look with pity at the young people being commissioned to conduct the reckless business of challenging spiritual forces. Mama Joe catches sight of Joe marching out with the others. After the commissioning prayer, Mama hurries to accost him, but he disappears from her view because the crowd is moving in different directions. She asks his siblings to find him, but none of them can.

Joe goes ahead of all the others. He runs home, procures an axe, and is already heading down to the foot of the hill. Nothing can stop him. He perceives no caution or challenge in his mission. He is sharp, very agile, and feels no resistance or fear. He is full of zest for life.

As Joe gets close to the shrine, he sees the priest of Ogwugwu, possibly making some incantations. Confident in his mission, Joe thinks nothing about the priest. He does not fear a dull priest who serves a dull god, but he slows down as he reaches the shrine.

The priest doesn't show any awareness that someone else is present; perhaps he is completely engrossed with whatever he is doing. His attention is focused on the deity, and he is muttering words and gesturing with his hands.

Joe stops and ponders the situation. Suddenly, deciding to proceed with his mission too, irrespective of the priest's mission, he stands next to the statue of Ogwugwu. It is a carved wooden image in the shape of a gong, though it also has human features. The image is entrenched on a raised platform inside a small hut with only a raffia roof on the top of four pillars. The statue is impaled on a fifth pillar in the centre of the hut.

The marvel of Ogwugwu is that it always looks polished, glistening under the brightness of the sun and moon. Ogwugwu has been here for as long as the oldest man in the village can remember. Some speculate about why the wood never gets old. Some say that each new priest makes a new image to replace the old one. This kind of information is a secret and cannot be discussed. No one cares to know the truth so the mystery of Ogwugwu will grow and its secret will continue.

Joe regards the image for a moment, then raises his axe to descend on it, in full view of the priest.

CHAPTER NINETEEN

Joe's raised axe descends on the image with the agility of youth. From the corner of his eyes, he sees the priest raise both hands and put them on his head, neither taking his eyes off the deity nor stopping his incantations.

The next minute, Joe sees his axe by his side and everywhere is dark.

Joe rubs his eyes to make sure he is not dreaming or falling asleep in broad daylight. After all, it's only 6:00 p.m. He jerks his head up, rubs his eyes again, and looks around. He can see light some distance away, like a shining flashlight.

This must be a bad daydream, he reasons. *Where am I? Why is it so dark around me?*

He feels his feet and they are able to move, so he walks in the direction of the light. He then bumps into a wall and finds himself sprawling across a wooden floor. He examines his sore forehead by rubbing it with his right hand. He senses no obvious bruises or blood from the impact. The pain quickly subsides.

Joe sits down and soaks in the situation. It occurs to him that he must have been caught in a trap. He looks around, especially towards the light, and sighs.

"I am in the darkest pit that can ever be," he murmurs. The distant light looks like an unsteady shining dot.

At that moment, the light seems to move up and shine on him through some unknown openings very high above. It is as though the light has spread around the pit and he can make out the shadowy walls,

made of concrete. He attempts to reach the light by climbing the pro-
truding concrete wall, but the hole through which the light shines seems
to recede. He gives up, because the more he tries, the more it recedes. He
is also cautious of hitting his head against another invisible wall; he senses
them all around him. He doesn't want to fracture his skull.

He reminisces about the last series of events in his mind. He remembers the message of the preacher, how he set off and headed towards
Ogwugwu's shrine with his axe, how he saw the priest standing in front
of the deity.

Where is the priest? he wonders. *Quickly, he swings around to see if the
priest is in the pit with him. He's unable to see anyone. The matter is clear: I am
imprisoned by Ogwugwu. But where? It is certainly at his shrine, but can that piece
of carved wood called Ogwugwu keep me imprisoned? Where exactly is this prison?*

At this point, Joe becomes very clear about the situation. The deity
has taken him and he cannot escape unless by God's powerful intervention. He is not afraid, but he is concerned about the implications. Is Ogwugwu more powerful than the God he serves? How can he escape and
be free again? What about his family, especially his mother? What will
be the fate of other believers if it becomes known that Ogwugwu has
imprisoned him?

He is not concerned about himself, but rather this crisis of faith. His
faith is badly shaken and he has no answers. He trembles at the implication of this incident becoming legendary, told over many generations.
He is sorry for bringing shame to the fledgling faith of his mother.

What if I never get out? he asks himself. *What will my local Christian
group do? How will this be explained to make sense to believers?*

The tragedy is more than he can bear. Stinging tears come to his
eyes. He musters all his courage and fights them back, because his mother
has taught him that tears never change anything. In fact, it is rare for
anyone in his family to resort to tears when faced with a challenge or
problem. They have been taught to look for solutions first.

*It's not just my challenge and shame, but that of my family, Christian friends,
and Ludu's community of believers. They may not be able to lift their heads again,
unless something happens, and urgently so as to reverse the situation.*

He thinks about praying, but he is too ashamed and confused to know where to start. He's not sure about where God stands on this matter.

"If only I know," he blurts out in exasperation. "If only I could think clearly and purposefully, I could know how to pray." He finally manages to gather himself together. "Oh God, I'm sorry for what I've brought upon myself and the shame I've brought to Your name. Please forgive me and help me."

CHAPTER TWENTY

With a dry throat, low energy, and poor morale, Joe is weak and vulnerable, but he tries to muster the courage to think calmly about his predicament and encourage himself through whatever means are available. He pictures his situation and determines not to suffer a double tragedy by suffering and dying like a coward without making any effort. He determines that even if he has been in the wrong and God seems to be angry with him, or has allowed Ogwugwu to imprison him, he will still call on the merciful God.

He speaks aloud his conviction: "God is the Father of all these spirits, and God of all flesh. He may hear me even this one time and set me free." He makes another attempt to pray coherently: "Oh God, You have been my Father since my father died, even though I didn't know You all the time. I want to understand what is happening to me. Do I have a chance here? Have I disgraced you? What has happened? Has Ogwugwu defeated You in my life? Can you hear me?"

More and more questions crowd his troubled mind. He wants to find out if God is angry with him. He wants to know what is keeping him captive.

Abruptly, he stops his questioning and reminds himself that mere questions will get him nowhere, even though his mind is filled with questions. He wants to ask more constructive questions, for that alone will get him answers that are relevant to his situation. He feels extremely frustrated, because his mind is unable to form questions that serve a useful purpose. Because he's not been receiving answers, he forces himself to stop asking.

He isn't sure how long his struggles will last. However, he looks ahead and, by means of the pinprick light, he sees people approaching. The light grows larger, but it's still not enough to enable him to see the exact shape of the dark pit. As such, he's unable to plan his escape.

The whole experience seems like a bad daydream. He senses that some of these newcomers may be his Christian brethren. He thinks that he can see Brother Goodnews leading them. They seem to be deep in conversation, but Joe is unable to hear them. He wants to move towards them, but he remembers hitting his head against the invisible wall. He simply waits and watches.

The people seem to walk in circles, disappearing and reappearing to his view every now and then. He's not sure how many they are, but he can hear low murmurs. He concludes that they may be praying.

From his estimation of time, this goes on for about an hour. He is comforted and encouraged, but also uncomfortable too, thinking that whatever forces are holding him should have been broken by now. He feels the anguish of imprisonment and loss of freedom.

He is engrossed with what he's seeing and feeling, excited at the thought of what the end of the matter will be like. When he no longer sees the ray of light or shapes of people appearing and disappearing, he wonders if he's been seeing a vision. He rubs his eyes.

I've been dreaming, he thinks. *Since when did I start dreaming while wide awake?*

He calms himself and begins to recite Bible verses, whichever ones come to mind. By so doing, he may receive the insight or counsel he desperately needs. He determines to speak out and not be silent, lest he waste away in this dungeon.

"If God be for us, who can be against us? On whose side is God? God is able to deliver to the uttermost they that come to Him by Jesus Christ. This God blesses even those that do not love Him. This God is God of all flesh and father of all spirits. This God will not allow injustice to be done even to the worst of humans. This loving, holy and most powerful God, do I know You? This God whose judgment is very deep, whose ways are past finding out, show me who You are and Your power to deliver. Let me know Your exceeding great power with which You raised Jesus from the dead. I'm almost being forgotten here. Please save me."

He gasps and breathes deeply, as though taking in the breath of life. He prolongs his exhalation deliberately, purging his system. Slowly and deeply, he senses hope and deliverance welling up inside. But the reality of his invisible imprisonment unexpectedly rises to swallow up the flicker of hope beginning to take form.

He reverts again to the awful feelings of frustration that are as strong as the walls of his captivity. He stops and decides to think slowly, to be calm and sort out his confusion in order to overcome it.

"I don't often understand all the ways of God," he muses to himself. "Will this force me to understand and appreciate Him? If that is the case, it may take my entire lifetime to unravel the mystery of God's thoughts and ways. I may even die here, unable to understand what went wrong. I thought I knew God in terms of what He wanted done, but I'm no longer sure, at least right now. I'm not sure I can hear His voice in this situation."

The thought of being alone, without any sense of God's presence, frightens him. He shivers as though someone has emptied a bucket of ice-cold water on him. He thinks about his shallow knowledge of God, reasoning that perhaps if he knew God deeply this would not have happened to him. He also nurses a secret fear that his faith might prove to be useless here in the territory of his enemy, Ogwugwu. In spite of his situation, he remains convinced that Ogwugwu is holding people's lives in captivity, regardless of the endless sacrifices poor people make to him.

I wish I could know what God is thinking about the situation, he thinks. *Is Ogwugwu being used by God to teach me lessons in practical faith?*

His heart pounds and he loses his composure again. Confusion creeps in. He pauses and takes a deep breath. First he has to purge all unhelpful thoughts. The worst thing would be to doubt himself and the existence of God. He breathes in and out in order to calm himself and think clearly.

Joe's concern hinges upon his desperate need to know how to handle the alienation he feels, the meaning and purpose of this situation. It is indeed a world where invisible forces impose themselves into the affairs of humans. No matter how humans try to organize their lives into a meaningful and logical order, these forces abruptly break every boundary and challenge their confidence in mastering the affairs of life.

The major issue is no longer Ogwugwu's dominion over the lives of the people but Ogwugwu's seeming dominion over his own life. He's disappointed about his weak faith.

"How can I come so far believing God only to now doubt my convictions?" he asks quietly. "I would rather that Ogwugwu exist than for me to not understand my faith anymore and lose confidence in expressing what I have believed and lived for. I hate this."

He feels as though he's been abandoned in a spiritual wilderness in order to challenge, re-evaluate, and re-establish his spiritual strength.

How is it that I've forgotten my mother and siblings and haven't considered what effect my actions might have on them? he wonders. *What are they thinking and doing right now?*

Worried, of course! They would all be worried about his safety and the damaging effect of gossip. His mother once had a strange encounter at a stream, not by choice; as for Joe, he deliberately walked into this confusion.

He feels very sorry for the pain he's bringing on his family. It hits him hard. For the first time, he weeps, for his heart is sorrowful. Hot tears run down his cheeks. He continues to weep until he no longer has the strength. He also feels hungry; he had hoped to break his fast after singlehandedly bringing down Ogwugwu. His plans and hopes are never going to be.

Weeping helps vent his emotion and to clear up his muddled thoughts. He is no longer agitated; his tears have washed away his fears, quelled his racing thoughts, and calmed his nerves. His mind is relaxed. After the storm of emotions, he feels a sense of calm.

Chapter Twenty-One

He hasn't figured out how he is going to get out, but he hopes for deliverance and peace. If Brother Goodnews has come with some believers to the shrine, it means that his family may have an idea about where he is. At this, he feels a degree of confidence and hope well up in him. Peace engulfs him. Though he can neither hear his mother's comforting words nor see God taking him out of this mess, he is not rejected; there is room for him to do better.

He doesn't pray, but he feels a presence surrounding him, birthing thoughts of prayer in his heart. He feels God is right there with him. He feels as though God's ears are close enough that he can whisper his prayers to Him. God has wrapped His strong arms underneath him. He feels comforted. He heaves a sigh of relief and triumph.

"Ask and it shall be given to you, seek and you shall find, knock and the door shall be opened to you," he speaks aloud. "Call upon Me in the time of trouble and I shall show you great and mighty things, which you have not known and you shall glorify Me. I have not said 'Call on Me' in vain. For we have a high priest who is touched with the feelings of our infirmities, so we can boldly come to the throne of grace to find grace and mercy to help in the time of desperation. The Lord in your midst is strong and He is mighty to save. Greater is He that is in me than he that is in the world."

These Bible passages race though his heart, bringing him hope, love, and courage. He feels free and enriched, conscious of the hope rising in his heart. He shouts out his favourite verse to his invisible captors: "Rejoice not my enemy for even though I fall I shall rise up again.

Though I'm struck down, I'm not destroyed; though cast down, I'm not abandoned; though I lose a battle, I am more than a conqueror; though wounded, I'm alive and well in His hands."

In a whisper, for there is no need to shout, since he already has God's attention, he is finally able to pray meaningfully: "Father God, thank You for forgiving me. You know I am truly sorry for my actions. I should have known exactly what You wanted me to do, and not become presumptuous about Your presence with me. I thank You for not abandoning me. I really appreciate the comfort You have brought to my heart in the midst of my desperation and hopelessness. I am sure You have also comforted my family and friends, especially my mom. Thank You, my Heavenly Father. You know I want to get out of this place. Please get me out. Help now! Oh Lord, help me! I vow to listen more and to understand what You want me to do than to act presumptuously. I submit to Your will and guidance. I thank You for hearing me…"

He continues to offer prayers of thanksgiving in confidence. Deep within him, he hears God speak His gentleness and quiet love: "Joe, I know you and I love you. I know your struggles, your actions, and your desires. I offer everything I have for you because you're the apple of My own eyes. You make mistakes, but no matter how low you feel or fall, I'll always be there to care for you and to help you. Understand my love, which is so abundant that you cannot outspend it. When you pass through the fire, look carefully and you'll see that I am there with you. My son, I love you and will help you."

Joe feels cradled in God's everlasting arms, filled with tender mercy, enlightening truth, joy, love, and hope. Without thinking about it, he attempts to rest his head against an imagined wall. He nearly falls over.

He stretches himself further and attempts to lean again. The more he stretches, the further the wall seems to recede. He keeps moving closer, sure that there has been a wall there; after all, was he not prevented from leaving the place by a wall? Did he not hit his head against a wall? Where is this barrier now?

He puts his hand forward, yet he cannot feel or touch any wall. He begins to walk, to run, to leap in the direction facing him, expecting to hit his head against the wall, as has happened before. He senses no wall.

He decides to move full speed ahead. He runs and runs until his heart races as fast as his feet.

The race fills him with strength and excitement. He is no longer worried, not when he has drunk of the rich tenderness that flows from God's breasts. The gentleness of God indeed makes Joe feel greater than he is, lighter than he has ever felt, and stronger than he ever imagined. He has not known love in this way—tangible, like the enveloping blanket that shuts off the winds of fear and frustration. He feels satisfied and full, and he wishes for this feeling to continue. He wants to leave a landmark for others so they will be able to find this kind of peace marked with serenity, love, and rejuvenation.

He stops running, but continues a brisk walk. His thoughts focus on this mysterious God who shows up when all hope is gone. His quiet prayers become a shout, for he is certain that he is free: "Oh God, thank You for setting me free. I want to get back to my family and friends. I want to apply what I have learned. I am set free to serve You better. You want me out there and not in here. You are with me wherever I am. God, I'm ready; let's start this race of life."

He picks up speed again, this time with assured strides and direction. His heart is changed, beating with passion and an attitude of mature courage and humility.

His pace is like that of a deer with the wind behind him. Only some hours ago, he was confused to the point of despondency. Now he feels the joy of being set free. He increases his momentum as though his swiftness determines the degree to which he will be separated from the undesirable life he is leaving behind. He races without any fear of hitting his head against invisible walls.

He sees light, then recognizes a footpath and takes it. He becomes more and more excited.

"Rejoice not, my enemy, for even if I fall, I shall rise up again, for my helper is my maker, and He is strong to save and to deliver," Joe screams with all his might, caring little if anyone is there to hear him.

CHAPTER TWENTY-TWO

N one of the other youth who embarked on the mission to rid the community of idols ventured near the shrine of Ogwug-wu. They restricted themselves to dismantling household charms and effigies. By the time they gather that night for prayers and to share testimonies of their exploits, it becomes obvious that Joe is missing. They are surprised that nobody went with him, and that he left all by himself to go to the shrine of Ogwugwu.

The only other group who exhibits the kind of faith as Joe exhibited goes to demolish the Sacred Pole beside the cave of the spirit with seven heads. The Sacred Pole is a gathering place for cult members after initiating new members. At the end of every outing, they return there to punish previous initiates who have renegaded.

The Sacred Pole lies in a valley surrounded by seven rolling hills, well hidden from outside view. The witches sometimes gather in their coven on the east side of the Sacred Pole, in an open field sheltered by surrounding thickets. The site is concealed so that no sound can be heard unless one is very close—and it's not possible for one to get close without being seen by the people in the valley.

The group that approaches the Sacred Pole is comprised of the leaders of the local church. They have no weapons and have gone in a team of seven. The valley is eight kilometres outside the town, and beside the Pole is an iroko tree which is also considered sacred. The tree is huge and old.

The team safely arrives in the valley, uninterested in demolishing the Pole but in nullifying its power. They circle the tree seven times, and then the leader of the group, Martin, asks everyone to join hands.

"Let every reinforcement from the four directions of the wind be cut off from you," Martin proclaims. He then asks everyone to stomp their feet on the dirt. "Let the sound from the stomping of our feet become a deep echo, reaching your roots to destroy its attachment to the ground for nutrients. We bring an end to your existence and nullify the stronghold you have had in people's lives. From today on, your power to keep anyone in bondage is broken. Your authority is nullified. The cries of people tortured at your base rise against you to bring your presence and existence to an end. We proclaim all this, believing that it shall come to pass in the name of Jesus Christ."

Everyone in the team shouts "Amen" at the top of their voices. They repeat the same for the Pole to destroy its foundation.

The Sacred Pole and the iroko tree have been a challenge to the Christians in Ludu, as some have been threatened with torture in the valley of the Sacred Pole. Some have previously been initiated into the cult. They became renegades when they turned to Christianity.

Because of the dread connected with this place and the rituals carried out here, no uninitiated person is able to go here and return safely without repercussion. It is said that if some renegades prove too tough, they can be sacrificed to the spirit living inside the Sacred Pole. However, no one has been sacrificed yet.

The team that went to the Valley of Sacred Pole returns safely. After the mission, they go to the school hall for prayers at 7:30 p.m. The prayer meeting is supposed to end at 9:00, but then they realize that Joe is missing. Some people go to see Mama Joe on their way to the prayer meeting; a few remain in their homes, not sure what to do.

The prayer meeting is supposed to be a time of praise and testimony, but Joe's disappearance casts a call over the event. It is nightfall and darkness is everywhere. Confusion and tension make the night even darker and drearier than it would ordinarily be.

CHAPTER TWENTY-THREE

Three hours pass and there's still no news about Joe. Mama has gone to see her older sister, Matilda, who lives close to the town hall. Matilda's son, John, ran breathlessly to call Mama Joe around 6:15, informing her that his mother wanted to see her immediately.

When Mama Joe arrives, Matilda breaks down in tears. She recounts to Mama Joe what Neme, the drunken priest of Ogwugwu, said in the market square, boasting about charming Joe and asking Ogwugwu to take him and never release him. "That boy is gone and Ludu is rid of him so that this land will rest," Neme had said.

"You mean that Joe has gone to the shrine of Ogwugwu to destroy it?" Mama Joe gasps in alarm.

"Yes, Neme said that Joe came with an axe to destroy the statue, but he was there to charm him. He boasted about possessing knowledge of many things ordinary people don't know. He claimed he knew before-hand that Joe would come."

Whatever Joe has done doesn't matter now to Mama. What matters is that she has to defend him. Like a mother lioness robbed of her cubs, she is furious and ready for a fight.

"If Neme thinks he can sacrifice my son to protect his god, then his god is a miserable and powerless god," Mama blurts in anger. She is enraged. "I will protect my son from them. If Ogwugwu is a god, let him fight for himself. If humans have to hurt, fight, or kill one another in order to protect a god's honour, he is not a god. So Neme is saying that he has sacrificed my son for the thonour of Ogwugwu? Why does Ogwugwu need Neme to protect him? Can he not rise and protect himself?"

"But is that not why Ogwugwu has a priest?" Matilda counters mildly. "Ogwugwu is a deity and needs to be served."

"Whether he's a deity or an idol, something is not sound there. Neme is saying that he needs to make incantations to enact Ogwugwu's personal protection of Ogwugwu by Ogwugwu?"

Matilda feels awkward about her sister's perspective. "I don't know, my sister. Don't ask me. I'm not Ogwugwu or his priest."

"Of course not, my dear. The point is that Neme's economic well-being is threatened. If Ogwugwu is no more, his financial security is gone. It's not just fighting for Ogwugwu, per se, as though Ogwugwu is anything beyond the demonic forces at work there, but Neme has his own vested interest in being the chief priest. He wants to take advantage of people's ignorance."

Matilda hasn't expected Mama Joe's anger towards Ogwugwu. She invited her so they could agree on how to go about looking for Joe, and negotiating with Neme. Though she feels the pain of the calamity that has befallen her sister's family, she is also afraid; mortals do not fight with gods. She doesn't know if Mama Joe's challenge to the priest of Ogwugwu while here in her house will bring a curse on her own household.

Mama Joe turns to her sister. "Did you say that Neme claimed to know ahead of time that Joe would go to the shrine of Ogwugwu?"

"Yes, that is what he said."

"Is Neme now a spirit that he claims to know things before they happen?" Without waiting for an answer, she continues, "All right, I'm going to his house to ask him where my son is."

All the time Neme has been in Ludu, he has never predicted anything that ever came to pass, for good or evil.

"It is said that where superstition exists, coincidence abounds," Mama Joe adds. "Rather than tell people he is afraid of losing his source of daily bread, Neme figured out that the program was geared toward cleansing the land. So he went there to make incantations. Of course he would claim that his incantations worked, since Joe is nowhere to be seen."

"You may be correct," Matilda concurs. "He came briefly to the arena when the preacher spoke. He then left quickly to gather his medicine bag. He said that he was determined to stay at the shrine to reinforce the powers of Ogwugwu, invoking a curse on any person who approached the image to destroy it."

That explains it, Mama reasons. *Ogwugwu has no power to protect himself, so he needs his priest to invoke demonic powers for him.*

"Thank you, Matilda. I have to go now. I'll think through these things and determine what to do. It's late now. Tomorrow I'll consult with some people. Who knows? Maybe Joe is already home, despite Neme's claims." Hope and faith rise in Mama's voice.

"Be careful, Keziah," Matilda cautions. "Don't do anything rash. One trouble is enough. You don't fight with spirits the same way you fight with humans."

"I hear you, my sister. Thank you."

"Remember, you can count on me to help so long as it's humanly possible. Eric will be home tomorrow morning. Both of us can support you."

Eric is Matilda's husband. He works with the local government as the finance director of the treasury. He's usually home on weekends.

"All right, my sister," Mama says. "The point is that spirits use humans to achieve their purpose. As for me, I'll put up a fight. I have a right to resist evil and challenge any unwanted situation in my life and family. But I hear you; I shall not do anything rash."

Mama gets up, gathering her purse and flashlight. She walks out of the parlour to the corridor that leads outside.

Matilda escorts her to the front courtyard. Even though Matilda isn't a worshipper of Ogwugwu, she wonders why Mama Joe persists in questioning the decisions of the gods.

"Sorry, my sister, I forgot to offer you something to drink," Matilda apologizes.

"Don't worry. This is not the time for food and drink. Next time. Good night, my sister. Don't be afraid for my family. What we need is prayer and God's intervention."

"Good night, Keziah. You've always been a strong woman, in the physical and the spiritual. Let not your strength and confidence fail you."

"It will not fail. I appreciate your support."

Mama Joe then leaves the compound, picking her way with the aid of her flashlight.

Chapter Twenty-Four

As Mama Joe walks away, she thinks about where to go. She feels like returning home and calling her children together for prayers. She needs quiet to think, for she is sure that many people from their Christian fellowship might have heard the news and flocked to her house. She will not be able to pray or think clearly in the presence of visitors.

She has feared for some time that Joe might run into serious trouble, because he is fearless, zealous, and eager to step out in faith. Joe was only eight years old when she found him commanding a guava tree to wither, just because the pastor had preached about faith. Joe takes the Bible literally.

Perhaps this experience will help him, Keziah reflects. *Oh God, I'm tired. I'm a widow who wants peace, but trouble keeps coming to me. Keep my son safe, I pray. Show Yourself as the God in this land, not Ogwugwu. Your name is at stake.*

She groans under the weight of the burden welling up in her heart and making her heart ache.

She is tired, but deep within her she has confidence that her son is safe. She's generally not afraid of spirits and their gimmicks; she thinks they behave like humans and can be negotiated with and appeased.

Her faith has brought about the salvation of her soul, but not for the destruction of demons or spirits. She is content just being a Christian and having hope of eternal life. It once seemed incomprehensible to ask God to give her a powerful faith so she could have whatever she requests in prayer, but she doesn't doubt the possibility of such faith anymore. She has often listened with wonder to Joe's stories about praying for people and seeing them get well, or needing something and seeing God provide it. She feels that such events are for younger people who have fewer responsibilities. Now that she sees herself in the fight, she must decide clearly the merits of faith.

She decides to go to the school hall rather than go home. She knows her children will be expecting her, but she wants to see if the people at the meeting will pray with her. She checks the time, and sees that it is 8:10. The meeting will be rounding off, but she decides to go anyway. Hopefully the leaders will know what to do about Joe's disappearance. It's not just a family problem; it concerns all Christians.

"If the preacher and leaders of the fellowship know how to stir up young people to challenge spirits, they should also know how to free them," she mutters to herself with a heavy heart.

Mama Joe has a way of seeing humour even in challenging situations, and that is how she manages to keep her soul afloat. At this point, she feels a degree of peace and confidence that all shall be well. She's also confident in the fact that she is not alone in this challenge. She imagines that the members of the fellowship will be there for her.

By the time she reaches the school hall, she is impressed to see many people. Some are standing while others sit in small groups, speaking in low tones. The mood is subdued and sober. There is no raised voice or laughter, even as the people catch sight of her walking towards the platform in the centre of the room.

As she looks around the room, she is encouraged that most of the people are still there. Seeing them gives her strength and assures her that she's not alone. She takes a vacant seat close to the front, to rest her feet, to think, and to pray.

Everyone is hushed. No one goes to her.

Stephen, the president of the local Christian fellowship, rises to his feet. "We're glad to see you, Sister Keziah. We were worried because the people sent to your house neither met you nor did your children know when you would be back. We need not tell the bad news; we are sure you know what has happened. Joe is missing, but we know where he is. We have bound ourselves together not to leave this place until he is restored to us. The good news is that Joe is alive and well."

"Amen!" everyone cheers.

When the noise dies down, Mama chips in. "Thank you, Stephen, and to everyone who has decided to fight this battle together with my family. I have come because I'm confident you will be ready to face this challenge with me."

"No need to thank us," Stephen says. "It is our business. Even though the prayer meeting has ended, we're not done yet. I sense there is already a positive shift in the spirit realm. Deliverance is already in motion for Joe, and therefore we must continue to contend for him. We serve a loving and merciful God. If Joe has missed something, some principle of spiritual warfare, God's mercy is enough to sustain and deliver him. Even more, God can teach him what he needs to learn in order to be victorious next time. We all learn from time to time, and God never tires of teaching us."

"Amen!" the audience roars again.

Stephen begins to coordinate the next stage of the meeting, which is most likely going to be an all-night prayer vigil. They sing many songs of praise.

As they continue to sing, with their local band leading the songs, the atmosphere begins to change. Their emotions, spirits, and thoughts soar, riding on wings of joy. They clap, jump, and feel elated.

When the session of praise ends, they pray for Joe in unison, asking for his immediate release. As they pray, people march up and down the aisle; some stand quietly while others gesture with their hands. They make their demands in prayer for more than thirty minutes.

After a while, they hear a shout. As the shout gets stronger, they recognize that the voice is Joe's. Suddenly Joe is before them, jumping and shouting on the podium. He is free!

A thunderous shout spontaneously breaks out in the hall. Everyone attempts to run to the front at the same time, each trying to be the first to embrace the newborn Joe, having emerged from womb of Ogwugwu. They push him over during the joyous stampede with laughter and shouts of praise.

Stephen intervenes, calling Joe up to the left side of the podium, and calls out a song:

The God of Abraham, Isaac, and Jacob
Jehovah, the Man of War
Your mercies endure forever and ever
Oh praise His holy name.

Joe has run all the way from the shrine of Ogwugwu, a long distance of ten kilometres. At first, he didn't know where he was going. He ran all the way, without taking time to note the distance. As soon as he saw the midnight lanterns outside the houses on the outskirts of town, he slowed his pace, concerned about stumbling over stones. However, his joy at being freed overtook his concern.

He decided to go immediately to the fellowship venue, believing that people would be gathered there to keep vigil on his behalf.

The songs, joy, and celebration of praise to God continue until everyone is exhausted. By the time they check the time, it is 1:00 a.m. on Saturday morning.

Chapter Twenty-Five

The capture and release of Joe dominates discussion in town the next day. Many people visit him to get the story firsthand. Even Neme, the chief priest of Ogwugwu, visits to confirm that the boy emerged sane, with no sign of mental disorder or wounds to his body. Neme goes away to tell people that he changed his mind and asked Ogwugwu to release Joe, believing that the young man had learned his lesson.

Brother Goodnews and his team conclude the evening meetings by Saturday night, leaving Sunday for worship and departure. The program is a success and revival breaks out among the people. More new people show up for the Saturday evening meeting than had come on Friday. Some of them attend out of curiosity to see Joe and confirm the story about him.

Events around Ogwugwu refuse to come to an end, however, because the parties involved are still intent on fighting the battle to assert who is the true God. They want to define the qualities of the God who should direct the affairs of the Ludu people.

Brother Goodnews goes with his team to the shrine of Ogwugwu early on Saturday morning. They speak to it, saying, "Every god who has not made the heavens and the earth shall perish from the surface of the earth and from under the heavens. Ogwugwu, have you made the heavens? Have you made the earth? If not, then perish."

Before leaving on Sunday morning, they again visit the shrine and address it as before.

Joe is determined to learn something and make the best of his experience. After he discusses his experience with the leaders of the fellowship, he refrains from discussing it further. He apologizes to the fellowship for the sorrow he caused them.

"I'm a modern day Jonah," he says, "but instead of being swallowed by a large fish, I was swallowed by a piece of polished wood."

People laugh at the absurdity of such a concept.

He becomes even more industrious and less boastful about his faith, though he is still zealous to preach. He is quieter at meetings, but not subdued. He listens more than he speaks. He gets up to pray at night, and during his spare moments he shuts himself up in his room and meditates upon God. He appreciates that God the Father, the Creator of the universe who sent Jesus to die for the sins of the whole world, is not a human being. He ponders about this God who is loving and forgiving and unlike the other deities worshipped locally. Individuals have used His name as a curse, challenged His authority openly, and even torn the Bible or burned it, yet He has not retaliated. He fights for Himself when He chooses to do so. He never sends people to kill one another to please Him. He is unique.

"The best I can do for myself is to know and understand Him on His own terms," Joe admonishes himself.

Seven days after the incident, the people living at the outskirt of the town tell a curious, sensational story about Ogwugwu. They say that he caught fire after terrible thunder and lightning struck his shrine. Neme was alerted, but before he could reach the shrine, Ogwugwu was nothing but ash.

Neme vows to make a new image, greater and deadlier than the first. He continues to work on this project month after month, even though it normally takes three months for new priest's to carve the image.

When six months have passed, the villagers wonder when the image will be finished. Nobody dares to ask Neme why it is taking so long.

Indeed, strange things are happening in the land. The older people of the town are thankful that they shall not live to see more desecration of the land, yet they are curious to see how these events will be resolved. They bury their unanswered questions in the wisdom of the elders: that which is hot will eventually grow cold.

CHAPTER TWENTY-SIX

In April of the following year, Joe's learns that he has gained admission to study law at the University of Nigeria, Enugu Campus. He applies himself to getting ready for postsecondary education. He has four months before school resumes.

On the opening day of classes, he travels to the school alone, refusing his mother's offer to travel with him. It is only a three-hour journey, and by 11:00 a.m. he arrives at the university. He pays his fees and gets a registration number as well as accommodation. By evening, he's settled into his own room.

He quickly decides which Christian fellowship to join. He becomes a member of the Christian Union, a member of the Nigerian Fellowship of Evangelical Students (NIFES). He goes on to become a member of the village outreach team, which goes out once every month for outreaches to neighbouring towns and villages. There are many mature Christian young people on the team.

Joe makes up his mind to learn the secret of the growth of mature leaders in the church, especially as it pertains to faith. When his diligence in studying the Bible and leading a God-fearing life gains him the respect of other members of the outreach team, the coordinator of the group gives him some responsibilities.

On one occasion, the coordinator has to attend an emergency General Committee retreat, and the mission team is supposed to leave for Okon that day for an outreach. The coordinator asks Joe to take charge of the team. Even though Joe has dreamed of advancing to this level of leadership, he didn't foresee that the day would dawn so soon. This is only his second semester as a first-year student.

He protests strongly, making the excuse that he's been in the group less than a year. His reasoning makes sense, because everyone is supposed to have been in the student Christian fellowship at least one year before being charged with the responsibility of leadership. However, the coordinator feels justified in making an exception because the outreach was planned three months ago. He encourages Joe and prays for him.

Joe spends the night praying with regards to the unexpected responsibility that has fallen on his shoulders. He feels peace afterward and is no longer agitated. He is among the youngest in the group, being only eighteen years, but the team members have confidence in him.

The next morning, the mission team sets out in the fellowship bus to Okon. They arrive the village at noon. Three young men and two ladies are awaiting their arrival at the town hall. When Joe and the others arrive at the town square, the local team joins them in the bus to lead them to their accommodations.

The local team of five people are the first converts of the new church from when the outreach group visited the year before. They formed a committee and have been working hard to build the village's interdenominational church ever since. Soon Joe and his team are able to rest, refresh themselves, and plan for the evening meeting.

While most members of the group are relaxed, Joe is restless. It's unusual for him to feel anxious about preaching or praying for people, but he has a lot of questions on his mind. What if the mission fails? What if something goes wrong? He cautions himself that the business is God's and that his part is to make himself available to God. Then he remembers the coordinator's admonishment: "God uses willing vessels, so become a willing vessel, then leave the rest to God." Joe feels peace return to his heart. He calls everyone together for prayers in preparation for the evening program.

CHAPTER TWENTY-SEVEN

At exactly 3:00 p.m., they leave for the town hall to set up their equipment and pray over the grounds in preparation for the program. On their way, they approach a clearing where somebody has used yellow virgin palm fronds to tape off the road. The implication is that the ground is sacred and shall not be crossed by anyone without proper rituals.

As the bus stops, Joe, sitting in the middle row of the twenty-four-seat bus, looks up to find out what the problem is. Ike, the bus driver, informs him that their way is blocked. Joe leans forward and looks ahead to the ceremonial roadblock.

Joe thinks for a moment. "Why, that's only a rope. Maybe some children were playing and forgot to untie a rope. After all, we passed here a few hours ago and there was nothing like this. Please, go ahead."

"We cannot go through that, Brother Joe," Ike says. "Look properly. That is not an ordinary rope. It is made from yellow virgin palm fronds. Whoever has put it there has something serious in mind to communicate. The rope indicates that the road is sacred, that crossing the rope will desecrate the place. Sure, we do not believe such superstitions, but the symbolism of this act sends a message."

"I don't like this," Joe says. "What kind of challenge is this when we've done nothing? What's going on? I just hope that…"

He sees a man emerging from a mud hut nearby. The man raises his hands to the sky and begins to say something which the bus passengers cannot hear.

Joe and Ike alight from the bus and meet the man ten metres from the bus. The man's hands are still raised and he's muttering to himself.

They bow their heads in respect and bid the man a good day.

"Can't you see? Can't you see? This road is blocked!" The man gestures with his right hand to the rope; his left hand clutches the lose end of the wrapper he's wearing.

"Sir, we can see," Joe says quietly, "but we need to pass though."

"Pass?" the man hisses. "All right, come and pass on the top of my head." He points to his head, which is covered with scattered white and brown curly hair.

"Please sir, allow us to pass. We don't know of any other road to the town hall. We are strangers here."

"I thought you knew everything. The people who sent for you should have known better. Nwokenku is not to be taken for granted. All I'm telling you is that you cannot desecrate my land. Go back to your school and study, for that is the reason your parents sent you there in the first place. Stop running around disturbing the deities my ancestors and elders revere."

The man named Nwokenku doesn't wait for their decision. He turns in fury and disappears into his hut.

The two young men get back on the bus to deliberate with the team. Nobody says anything, as they're all engaged in speculative thoughts about Nwokenku's challenge. Their confidence and peace about bringing the good news to the people is shaken. No one wants to say anything unless they're sure it will help the group make sense of this unexpected challenge.

"So our presence is deemed a confrontation to the deities even though we're here to pray for people who need help, and preach to those who want the good news," Joe says reflectively. "We've come in peace, not to desecrate the land, as we're not going to force anyone to listen to us. But forces we can't see are already incensed against us. No wonder it is said that we wrestle not against flesh and blood but against principalities, powers, rulers of the present world, and spiritual wickedness in high places. I encourage us to be careful and to act wisely. We are in a battleground."

Everyone is quiet, judging the full import of the decision they must make.

"Should we go back to the campus as Nwokenku advised us?" Joe asks, looking closely at two of his closest friends, Vincent and Monica. "Or should we proceed on our mission?"

He hears no responses. Even Vincent and Monica are thinking and weighing their response.

Joe's experience with Ogwugwu is still fresh on his mind. The wisdom he's gleaned has made him cautious when it comes to dealing with unseen forces. Beside him, his friend Vincent lifts his eyes.

"We cannot afford to go back to the university without executing the purpose of our mission," Vincent says. "It'll be a huge disappointment to the program organizers and will discourage everyone."

"Going back will also dampen our faith," Monica points out.

The general consensus is that two volunteers from the group shall go out and take down the rope.

Monica and Vincent volunteer. They carefully untie the rope from one side, then call for Ike to drive through. Once the bus has passed, Vincent ties the rope back in place. He and Monica get on the bus again, wondering if Nwokenku is watching them or not.

They drive to the town square. No voice or sound is heard; no door is opened and no human comes out. Everyone is silent and focused to avoid distractions and unnecessary comments.

Though Joe feels calm and unperturbed as they arrive at the town hall, a degree of uneasiness creeps in. His thoughts go wild about what might happen. He wonders about the encounter and what kind of spirits are operating in Okon. He wonders whether the man who challenged them is the chief priest of some deity who caught wind of their coming and is prepared to oppose them.

He knows there is no going back. Encountering contrary forces is inevitable in any mission of significance. The important thing is that he needs to be prepared for a possible confrontation. He calls the team together and leads them in a prayer walk of the town square. They go from singing and clapping into prayer. They pray for the success of the program. Within an hour, they finish and are ready to begin the program.

They go on to invite people, moving from house to house. At 5:30 p.m., the band, hired by local organizers, blasts music from loud speakers.

The people sing, dance, jump, and feel excited. Many young people from the village begin to come around. Older people arrive, too, and take the seats arranged at the centre of the square.

At 6:30 p.m., Joe is called up. He introduces himself briefly and talks about forces that can hold people captive. His text is from John 8:32–36. He dwells on empowerment through knowledge of the truth. For the past months, he's been studying how spiritual empowerment comes through knowledge.

"Ignorance and presumptions are bedfellows capable of stagnating one's life to the extent that such a life becomes a dumping ground of evil things. Such a life will be unproductive. I'm sure you don't want your life to be a refuse dump, do you?"

"No!" the people chorus.

"Neither does God intend that to be your experience."

He uses practical examples from everyday life to show that if one doesn't know what God says about one's life, one can become unmotivated and unproductive.

"What you don't know is bigger than you, but God wants you to know Him so that He can empower you to overcome the situations that intimidate and oppress you. You cannot put a brake on life, but you can set boundaries according to your knowledge. Is that not why Jesus died, so that we might have power to experience the love of God in fullness? From that experience, we can impact other people's lives through love. A deceived person becomes a victim and a loser. Go for the freedom Jesus has provided. As the Son of God, if He sets you free tonight, you shall be free indeed."

He surveys the faces of the people as he preaches. Some are pleased and enthralled. On the whole, everyone is quiet. It may be his youthfulness, conversational tone, and participatory invitation that captivate them. Or he may be making sense and touching their hearts with the good news.

He continues with renewed vigour. "Any inheritance that is not possessed is useless. I am here to remind you that this is the time to enter into the divine inheritance Jesus purchased for you when He died on the cross. Begin to reconstruct the reality you want to have. I invite you all now to come forward and make a decision to identify with the man, Jesus, who shall change your lives and commission you through the power of the Holy Spirit."

He beckons to the audience with his hand. Nobody stirs. He repeats his call several times, until one little girl, about ten years old, steps forward. Soon a woman joins her at the front. Others begin to make their way to the front. Meanwhile, soft music plays. He finally stops the music and prays for the people at the front. When he's finished, he calls for counsellors to talk with them individually.

To Joe, the evening turns out to be greater than he anticipated. Fifty new people have decided to follow Jesus.

The meeting confirms to Joe what it means to be a willing and relaxed vessel and to act with fervour and confidence on the word of God while trusting the Holy Spirit to do what He wants to do.

Most of the team members spend the rest of the meeting counselling people and praying for their specific needs.

That night, as Joe goes to bed, he feels like a new man who suddenly understands a mystery that has been shrouded in dim light. He is a brand new person, experiencing his own deliverance from the secret tension he has about faith.

"This is peace," he muses to himself.

Seeing such a large number of new members is encouraging to the team members. On Sunday morning, they conduct a worship service. They then leave Okon at noon to return to the university, hoping that they'll be able to meet up with the afternoon fellowship meeting on campus.

They are very happy for bringing joy to the people of Okon. Many people have testified to receiving salvation, healing, deliverance, and the baptism of the Holy Spirit.

Joe's experience and growth persists. He will be an instrument to help others who have struggled. He's positioning himself to help people who may be confronted by similar conflicts.

CHAPTER TWENTY-EIGHT

Caroline is on her own in the confectionery business, without any further support or partnership with Mama Joe, yet her financial success is unabating. A loan from her brother boosts her confidence, and she and Onyema decide to rent a bigger shop in the market square to enable them to stock more goods. They open their store for as many days of the week as they want. Every so often, she receives orders from people to make cakes or meat pies. However, Mama Joe continues to dominate the field because of her years of experience and unsurpassed generosity towards her customers. Notwithstanding, the market is robust. People are developing an appetite for baked goods and the convenience of ready-prepared food.

Since Caroline announced to Mama Joe that she would no longer attend church, she hasn't had any further discussion with her. Sometimes she allows her children to go to church, but she doesn't go herself. As far as she can see, she is making tremendous progress in her business, hence it wasn't a bad decision to leave the church.

Onyema is also fully involved in the business. He is responsible for purchasing their goods from Onitsha. The family is able to make ends meet and pay their children's school fees promptly. Long ago, they paid Mama Joe back for the loan she gave them to help with their son's school fees.

During his biweekly trip to Onitsha, Onyema secretly wishes he'll run into Mr. Unna, so as to give him a piece of his mind. He would then make sure the swindler paid back the money he took. Unfortunately, both the girl at the restaurant and Mr. Unna seem to have vanished into thin air. Nobody at the restaurant can recall seeing such people there.

Onyema is determined to see that their years of being cheated are over. He decides to travel to Lagos as well to buy wares. His tenacity and business acumen have helped to grow their supermarket business. Caroline, a very pleasant woman, has excellent customer service skills. In fact, she offers small gifts and extra discounts to their regular customers to show appreciation for their patronage.

Upon coming out of his emotional hibernation, Onyema starts to visit the palace of the village chief, Donatus Onwendi, and the two men begin to develop a personal friendship. Caroline even notices that some evenings, soon after supper, Onyema leaves to go to the palace. She says nothing about it or tries to find out what he does there. As usual, they freely share information, but when one of them feels like staying silent, the other respects that and waits until he or she is ready to talk. Caroline has so many things she's focusing on that she's not particularly interested in knowing what Onyema does at the palace. In her imagination, it must be something to help grow their business.

Onyema also begins to build friendships with members of the community. He attends his clan's local council meeting. Most of the time, the men gather in the evening to talk about affairs in the village, sharing their opinions about everything.

"Things are changing in this land," the oldest man, Ikeaza, says during a meeting. "That Joe, whom I knew when his father was born, dared Ogwugwu and still emerged sane. It's incredible. We are fast losing control of our lives, I must say. I don't have many more years left to live; I'd sooner die and be spared from seeing further desecration of our sacred land and the confusion that shall be unleashed upon the living as a result of this kind of effrontery."

"Power is everything," says Chief Onwendi. "Whether it is economic, physical, or spiritual, you cannot do without power, not to mention money. The gods fight for control of their territories just as humans fighting over positions. Ikeaza, though you are old, the deities are challenged before your very eyes in ways we have never seen before."

"I'd rather fight them with everything I have than watch and do nothing," Ikeaza says.

Onwendi nods. "There goes the warrior spirit of our fathers. Ikeaza, the warrior who never turns back until the last enemy is on the ground! We may need more than our warrior spirits to make meaning out of these onslaughts. The battle lines are no longer straight and clean. They are intermingled with unseen forces and people beyond Ludu."

"You are correct, my son," Ikeaza says. "But it's our responsibility to recreate the meaning of our traditional beliefs for future generations."

"Yes," Onwendi observes. "That's why we maintain our communal connections, so that we can heal and grow together. Is it not said that together we stand, but divided we fall? I feel sorry for those who are alone. We cherish the thing that binds us together—and that is our culture."

Onwedi's granduncle was the first chief of Ludu. The British government instituted him. Before that, Ludu was ruled by a group of elders, the Ndi Ichie, facilitated by the chief elder from the lineage of the oldest son of the founding father of the Ludu people.

Onyema enjoys such interactions and goes home more focused and inspired about how to rebuild his family's fortune.

Caroline gradually realizes that their thriving business must be as a result of Onyema's community activities. Even though he doesn't tell her what he does when he's out, from experience she recognizes the blessing of such outings and is well-pleased. Onyema is a likeable young man with a wide range of experience in business and politics. Other community members appreciate his insight. Chief Onwendi likes him very much, and is ready to tap into his wealth of knowledge by involving him in community projects.

CHAPTER TWENTY-NINE

Most Fridays, Onyema and Caroline take time off from manning the store to do inventory and bookkeeping. After working for a while in silence, except in response to questions or comments related to the work at hand, at 1:20 Onyema announces to Caroline that he has a special meeting with the chief at 2:00 p.m. He tells her that Onwendi needs his help with his timber business, and that he wants to offer him work as an independent consultant, not an employee. He informs her that he'll be visiting her brother in Onitsha the following week.

"What do you want to discuss with Obinna?" she asks.

"I thought you knew. Don't you think I need to do something more than running the supermarket? I think it's time to revamp our import business.

"Yes, it's long overdue."

"The business you've grown has helped our family survive, and it meets our short-term needs—but not our long-term ones. I've waited too long to take the lead."

Onyema isn't a man of many words. Before he says something, he thinks it through. Therefore, Caroline understands that this decision is as good as done. She's been quite strong for her family, but she's relived that Onyema is finally picking up the gauntlet. It's what she's been hoping for and longing to hear for a long time.

So this is how our years of poverty will be forgotten, she thinks. *Our ashes will turn to beauty and my heavy heart will lighten with joy, once again attuned to songs of leisure. Onyema, my very own, is roused like a lion, wakened from his slumber as a strong man ready to fight his enemies.*

Her dreams of living in luxury return. She'll no longer feel intimidated in Ogochukwu's house. Perhaps they will even be able to move back to Lagos. Now that they've been twice swindled, they'll never fall into their clutches again. As the elders say, "When a tropical fire ant stings you, you learn shrewdness so that the next time you sit on the floor, you shall sit with discretion."

Onyema doesn't wait for her to respond because he understands that she'll need time to digest the news. He goes into the bedroom to get ready for his meeting with Chief Onwendi.

She follows him in and watches as he dresses. Love and pride well up in her for the man she has always believed in. She crosses over to him and stands before him by the door to their wardrobe.

When Onyema stoops to tie his shoelace, he looks up to find Caroline watching him tenderly. He understands this look, especially the pride and love in her eyes. He begins to regret the years he has wasted. He falls in love with her anew and determines even more strongly to make up for his past failures.

Without saying anything, each understands what the other is thinking. The silence brings rich comfort, like a calm and reassuring stream after a raging storm. The revelation ushers in healing and brightness.

"So long, Onyi, I didn't think we'd come to realize all that we've sacrificed in each other," Caroline finally whispers.

Onyema still feels guilty for his pessimistic attitude towards their misfortune. Caroline reads the self-condemnation in his eyes and is determined not to allow it to go on. Seizing the moment to heal together, she reaches out and wraps her arms around his neck. Without words, she leans against his chest and begins to weep.

The tears don't surprise Onyema. This is the woman he's known for years, the wife he married, the lady of his heart. This is the mother of his children, the queen of his world, and she is very sensitive to his feelings. He's ravished by her love, ashamed for how he has let her down through resentment. He understands her and realizes how deeply he loves her, even more for reminding him about the strength he possesses as a man, a husband, a lover, a friend, a father, and a leader who will birth new vision for the family.

He holds her close and leads her towards the edge of the bed, sitting her down gently. He kneels before her and kisses away her tears. He caresses her face while looking deeply into her face with tenderness. Onyema lifts her up, carrying her in his arms and smiling down at her. He puts her down on the bed.

The residue of the troubles that have stalled their marriage give way in a single moment by the strength of their conjugal union. All is in the rapturous state of their love. They make love, peace descending on them. When their love is satisfied, they fall asleep in each other's arms.

CHAPTER THIRTY

At 3:30, their bedroom door is still closed. The world seems to have come to a stop through their total abandonment to each other. Caroline hears their children playing outside, rousing her to the reality of daily life. The children have been back from school for more than an hour, she realizes.

She dresses and wakes Onyema, who has been basking in deep sleep. He slowly opens his eyes and remembers his appointment with Onwendi. He dresses quickly, already late for the appointment. He wonders what explanation will suffice.

"What shall I tell the chief?" he asks.

Caroline offers to go with him so to explain that she had requested Onyema help her with something, that it was her fault.

Onyema isn't in the habit of using his wife as an excuse. He should be able to take the blame as a man, especially now that he's making an effort to be the responsible leader of the household. He decides to go alone and trust his wisdom to know what to tell Onwendi.

Onyema arrives at the palace by 4:00, but Onwendi is busy in a meeting. In fact, Onyema has to wait for two hours before he is able to meet with the chief.

Finally, when he goes in, Onwendi apologizes for keeping him waiting. He's been very busy with emissaries from three neighbouring towns ever since the morning. Onyema is thankful for these unexpected meetings, as they make it unnecessary for him to apologize. The timing has been perfect.

Onyema has been making himself useful to Onwendi by helping him manage some highly sensitive administrative responsibilities. The chief has also been thinking about how to help Onyema get back to his import business. Onwendi is a joint owner of the local timber company and wants Onyema to become a sales representative. He's convinced that Onyema's entrepreneurial skill and experience will help revamp the company and attract new customers.

"I really thank you for considering my involvement in the timber business," Onyema says.

"All right," says the chief. "What do you think of becoming a sales rep?"

"I have considered your offer, and it is very good, but I have decided to return to my import business in Lagos. I'm thinking of moving my family back there, since the government has relaxed its regulations."

Onwendi smiles. "I'm happy to hear that you're finally picking up the shards of your broken business pot. My man, that is the best thing for you. But I'll still need your help in revamping my timber business."

"Certainly. I'll gladly do the best I can while I'm still in Ludu. Even once we return to Lagos, I'll still visit from time to time if need be."

"You're exactly the kind of young man we need in this community."

"It's my pleasure," Onyema says, "and I thank you for the opportunities you've given me. Now, you've had a busy day and I must be taking my leave so you can have some rest. Let's plan to meet again to discuss the details of my role in your company.."

"You're right, I do need some rest. Let's plan to meet in the next two weeks. I'll check to make sure I don't have any conflict this time."

Onyema bows low. "Chief, may you live forever."

"You too, my friend." He pats Onyema's bowed head with the fan in his hand.

Onyema travels to Onitsha two days later to discuss with his brother in-law his intention to return to business. Obinna is very pleased with the idea and agrees to help him secure a business loan. Onyema shows him a three-year plan for rebuilding the business, and part of the plan is to open a boutique in Ludu in the next year. In the first and second years, he'll continue to help Caroline run the supermarket and work with Onwendi as an independent sales consultant. He'll make sure their supermarket continues to generate enough profit to meet their immediate needs so that the business loan can go towards re-establishing the import business. He'll use the third year to find a strategic location in Lagos and find new partners to work with him. This time, he's determined to never send money to any middleman. If he has to, he'll go to Taiwan himself every time to purchase goods.

CHAPTER THIRTY-ONE

Three months later, Caroline finds out that she's pregnant, and the discovery adds fuel to their love. They've already picked a name for the baby. If it's a boy, he'll be named Ositadinma; if it's a girl, she'll be named Nkeiruka. The pregnancy brings more gaiety to their relationship, as they've hoped to have a fourth baby.

Caroline isn't the type to suffer from morning sickness, but as she enters her fifth month of pregnancy, she notices that her energy level gets lower as the day passes. Onyema is very worried, because his wife doesn't usually have difficult pregnancies.

This pregnancy is unlike the others in many respects. Caroline hasn't been sleeping well, and she often has strange dreams about fighting with someone over her unborn baby. She expresses her fears to Onyema, who initially blames it on her anxiety and excitement about the future. However, Caroline thinks the issue goes beyond ordinary anxiety. She doesn't know where to turn for help except to brace up and hope that her condition improves soon.

Going to see a doctor doesn't help. The doctor's only suggestion is that they go for a long walk every evening to relax her mind and muscles. The walks help a little bit in easing her discomfort, but she soon begins to lose her appetite, too. The doctor carries out further tests, which reveal nothing. Finally, in order to minimize Caroline's stress due to lack of sleep, the doctor prescribes sleep medication. The medication works the first two nights, but from the third night her case becomes worse. The medicine only makes her drowsy. Sometimes she can hear voices talking to her, but she can't remember the discussions. The doctor advises that she stops the medication altogether, because it hasn't helped and may affect her baby if she forms the habit of taking it. She discontinues the sleeping pills.

With time, Caroline's sleep begins to improve but she still wakes up several times per night for no reason. She decides to contain her difficulty as best as she can. She faithfully attends the antenatal care clinic and talks less about her challenges.

Onyema is greatly affected by his wife's situation. He experiences a conflict between spending time on the business and spending time with his distressed wife. A pregnancy that should be their greatest source of joy turns out to be a source of distress.

CHAPTER THIRTY-TWO

"I'd rather have my baby alive than dead," Caroline says in her sleep.

Onyema is woken by her voice and watches as she argues with someone in her sleep. After listening a while, he decides to wake her up. He shakes her, but she continues to talk with her eyes shut.

"This time, I won't agree with you," she murmurs. "This baby is significant to my husband and me. We've been wanting to have a baby girl. No, I'd rather have her alive than dead."

Onyema is confused and wonders about the meaning of this argument. He shakes her more firmly. Slowly, she half opens her eyes, but closes them again and continues to talk: "I think it's time we define our relationship. You cannot tell me that it's either my life or the life of my baby. No, no. I question your authority. You want to kill us because I won't give her up?" She becomes silent for a while. "I know you've been revealing things to me, but this is different."

"Caroline, stop!" Onyema snaps. "What are you talking about?"

Startled, Caroline opens her eyes wide, then sighs and looks away.

Onyema rises from the bed and pulls her up. "Please, tell me. Who were you talking with and what was it about your life and our baby?"

Caroline begins to sob with despair. She is unable to gather her thoughts to form words, for it's become clear to her that she's fighting an invisible enemy. Onyema cuddles her to calm her down and she leans on his chest.

She continues sobbing, her breathing getting lower and softer, and then she falls asleep in her husband's arms.

Onyema is surprised at how peacefully she sleeps now. He eases her back onto the bed and watches her for almost an hour. Feeling sleepy himself, despite all his burning questions, he succumbs.

He wakes up a couple of times to check how she's doing. Every time, she's sleeping so peacefully that she doesn't turn or move from where he set her down. He concludes that whatever his wife encountered must be a blessing in disguise, for she's having her most peaceful sleep in months. He can't remember the last time she slept for three hours in a stretch.

At 6:30 a.m., Caroline is still sleeping. Onyema leaves the bedroom and attends to the children, helping them and making sure they get some breakfast before heading off to school.

Finally, at 9.30, Caroline stirs. She looks refreshed; the lines around her eyes are gone. Despite being pleased about her peaceful sleep, Onyema bides his time in asking her about the experience last night. He is very eager to hear Caroline talk about the encounter she had with the invisible presence, and he wonders whether the story will negatively impact her seeming tranquillity and peace of mind.

From all indications, Caroline isn't ready to discuss the event of the previous night. Onyema tries to draw her into a discussion by asking how she feels, but her only response is that she feels fine. Finally, he asks if she wants to go for a walk that evening. Caroline doesn't seem interested.

Onyema is worried. Normally Caroline loves to walk with him, and they're free to talk about anything, whether serious or just friendly chatter.

He decides to visit some friends after lunch. Caroline seems not to care that Onyema is going out. Onyema hopes that by leaving her alone, she might be able to sort out her thoughts and be in a communicating frame of mind when he returns.

No matter how long she delays this discussion, he thinks, *I'm determined to have it.*

Onyema returns after one and half hours. Though she feels strong, she seems not to be herself. She's hardly able to hold any conversation for more than five minutes without feeling distracted. She often stares vacantly and shakes her head at nothing. But as evening wears on, she seems more relaxed and focused. She even helps get dinner ready.

After the children are sent to bed, Onyema lingers with her in the living room. She is quiet and reserved and not showing any sign of sleep. Onyema is too tired to keep awake, having not slept well the previous night, so he finally suggests they go to bed. He's unsure of what the night may hold.

As soon as they settle into bed, Caroline takes his left arm and slips it under her left side; she pulls his other arm over her chest. She squeezes her feet into his and snuggles as close to him as she can.

Now that she feels relaxed and secure, she begins to talk.

Onyema is pleasantly surprised but appreciative of the ease with which she speaks. She reminds him about her relationship with the spirit woman, whom she's known since her teenage years. She has told Onyema several times how the woman used to visit her in dreams to reveal things to her. Onyema has heard this part of the story before, especially the time when the woman had instructed her to stop working for Mama Joe.

"You mean to say that this is the woman you were arguing with last night?" he asks.

"Exactly! She was telling me that I'd have a baby girl, but that she would die. When I protested and told her she had no right to tell me that, she mocked me, laughing and saying that she had a right to determine what happens to me. She informed me that I could either choose for the baby to live and I die, or that I live but the baby dies. I reminded her of her advice not to work for Mama Joe anymore in exchange for surviving future pregnancies. Why would she suddenly change the agreement after I had obeyed her? It was a long argument. I was adamant that my baby and I both live. I made it clear that our family has come a long way, and I wouldn't accept such adversity. The spirit woman said that I couldn't have my life and my baby's, and she threatened to deal with me for daring to challenge her authority."

Onyema is surprised and angry at how this strange woman is bargaining for the life of his wife and unborn baby. He remembers also that the many things the woman has revealed have come to pass. He has neither encouraged nor discouraged Caroline from this relationship. Initially he thought that the relationship was ordinary and might even be beneficial. He reasoned that having a form of spirituality could give one a glimpse into the unknown. Isn't that better than just having religion? Now he sees the whole picture; this spirit woman is like a creditor knocking on their door to demand a pound of flesh in exchange for services rendered. He sighs, unable to understand it.

He feels mocked by his helplessness to save his wife and unborn baby from a furious spirit. He gazes vacantly into the dim darkness. Does he believe in spirits? He has never believed in their power to influence or afflict. Regrettably, it's no longer a question of whether he believes in them or not. The question is now: how could he have all these good things and not pay for them one day?

Caroline is surprised that he doesn't say anything in response to her story. She shakes him. In response, he sighs and takes a deep breath. He wishes this spirit woman would demand money instead of the life of the dearest people in his life.

"Life is a tragedy," he mutters, shrugging his right shoulder, "and complication and confusion are its messengers."

He has always been a strong, determined, and courageous person, but this new development sends cold chills down his spine.

If you're fighting with someone visible, at least you can know where to strike a blow and how to dodge one. But when you fight with someone you cannot see, you're like meat in the stomach of a vulture.

Finally, he clears his throat. "Caroline, I want you to be courageous. When you find yourself in the midst of battle, you have to fight or be killed. Even though this woman has started the fight, remember that it's not the first person to throw a punch who wins. Now that you've started to fight back, I'll join forces with you. Together we shall overcome."

Caroline smiles. "I agree with you. Initially, I was afraid, but no more."

He gives a short, low laugh, summoning up all his manly courage. His laughter seems to him unreal and unconvincing, but it suffices to encourage Caroline and bring a smile to her lips.

Embracing her, they lay still; the only sound is their breath. They sink into sleep when they have exhausted their thoughts.

Some minutes past 7.00 a.m., Onyema opens his eyes and notices that Caroline is still sleeping. He lies still for a while before disengaging himself from her embrace. Their children have left for school without waking them.

CHAPTER THIRTY-THREE

At 9.00 a.m., she is still sleeping. He wakes her up so that she can get ready for her appointment at the antenatal clinic. She's able to make the appointment on time and the report is encouraging. Her due date is October 30, in exactly two months and five days. She is doing well health-wise.

Night after night, her quality of sleep improves and her energy level increases. The couple is very much impressed at the sudden improvement. They neither talk about the previous strange encounter nor seem interested in talking about it. However, Caroline has a feeling that the spirit woman's threat still hangs over them, and that she may be busy scheming an unexpected attack.

She decides to confide in someone about the strange encounter. Ordinarily she would go to Mama Joe, but she feels Joe is the right person to talk to. Despite having cut off contact with Mama Joe, she feels this situation is serious enough to swallow her pride. She keeps her ears and eyes open to learn when Joe is back from school.

Two weeks later, she hears that Joe is home for a short break. Her next plan is to find an evening when her husband is occupied outside of the home so she can visit Mama Joe's house. Three days later, an opportunity comes knocking. Onyema has to go see Chief Onwendi for an important committee meeting. She dresses quickly and leaves the house.

Mama Joe is home. Caroline greets her and apologizes about the past, but explains that things aren't going well with her, especially with her condition. She doesn't dwell on the suddenness of her visit. She inquires if Joe is in. She briefly reminds Mama Joe about the spirit woman, and Mama is sympathetic, assuring her that she's taking the right step by seeking support.

Joe is in his room studying when Uju comes to announce that he has a visitor. Joe then meets Caroline in the parlour. He is very happy to see her even though he's curious to know why she has come.

Without further ado, Caroline narrates the story about her relationship with the spirit-woman. Joe is surprised that she has come to him because he knows that the couple prides themselves on being agnostics. He knows that she stopped working with his mother in conformity with this same spirit woman's directives.

"What do you want me to do?" Joe asks.

"I don't know exactly, but I feel you may be able to help me understand the meaning of what's going on."

"From your story, it seems as though this woman is demanding payment for the free services she has been offering to your family all these years. The payment she demands is your complete subservience, without any questions. It's an indisputable law that a worker deserves her wages, and spiritual laws are not easily broken without repercussion. Remember that the one you choose to obey holds the rulership of your life."

The truth of Joe's words hit Caroline like a bolt; she's never thought of the spirit woman's demands in such serious terms. She has been a parasite, and now the day of reckoning has come.

She is speechless. Joe waits patiently for her to respond.

"I really regret my ignorance," Caroline says after a moment. "I can only ask you to help me deal with the matter. I have no idea how to handle it."

"The only thing I can promise is to pray for you privately, and in cooperation with a couple of my close friends. That is simple but very crucial. We need to invite God into this matter. You have to return to God through repentance."

"I guess that's why I came to you," Caroline says with hope and confidence rising in her voice.

"The battle lies with you. You will be responsible for breaking the bond between you and this spirit woman. I must warn you that it's not going to be easy. It's a race for life, but with God on your side, you will be victorious. You'll need support to win this battle."

Caroline knows he's speaking the truth, but she's sad at how she underestimated the degree of damage this supposedly innocent relationship could do to her family.

"There is something you can do to be strong and resist this woman," Joe announces after thinking for a while.

Caroline is all ears. "I'm willing to do anything!"

"It's simple. Now, think about this: if two people are fighting, one of them is your friend and the other is your enemy. Will you help your enemy or your friend?"

"I will help my friend."

"Good, Caroline, good!" Joe exclaims. "God has to be your friend, so you can draw support from Him in order to defeat this creditor who is holding you captive."

"How will I be able to do that?"

"Tell God that you want Him to be your Father and friend. Tell him that you're returning to Him through Jesus Christ. Let Him know that you're sorry for ignoring Him and departing from Him. Ask him to forgive you. Do this and let me know how you fare afterward. I want you to do this after thinking through it privately. I'll see you when I visit again next month. Whatever is to be done, do it immediately. You don't know how soon your attacker will return to make good on her threats."

Joe doesn't talk about his encounter with Ogwugwu except when he wants to use it to help others who find themselves in spiritual quagmires.

"Of course, you know about my experience with Ogwugwu," he continues. "There are many things we don't know about spiritual dynamics and how our choices affect us. The good news is that we're never written off. It's not too late to lay the foundation of your success on Jesus Christ, the Son of God. If you want to be on the list of winners in this battle of life, you need the power that comes from an experiential knowledge of the friend who sticks closer than a brother—Jesus. You need to speak up and bind the strongman who seeks to rule your life against your will. To do that, you need God on your side. Whether you'll win or lose depends on how you follow Him. When you accept God's offer, you become a mighty soldier who cannot be routed. You overcome because Jesus is actively living inside you and is for you. With that unity, you cannot be destroyed, because ignorance and foolishness is done away with. I tell you, the wisdom I gained from being delivered from Ogwugwu have encouraged me so much and given me faith and confidence to stand up to situations and believe to see more victories."

"It's interesting that you see something positive from the experience," Caroline says.

"Yes. There's always something positive in what God allows to happen to His children. You can be sure that something good will come out of your own experience if you are humble enough to learn from your mistakes. I tell you, at the end of all this, you'll become a better person than you were before. Now, let me read you a poem I wrote about having God as a friend:

Everyone needs a friend.
Have you ever hit rock bottom in life and went morose with rejection?
Have you ever hit the skies so you would go crazy with joy?
Have you ever hit the whirlwind and been enveloped in a cloud of confusion?
Have you ever hit the thick dark fog on your highway of life?
Have you known the dark cloud of monsoon like old bones?
Have you been in the smoke that nearly chokes life out of you?
Have you ever been caught in the Harmattan wind, naked?
I've been there.
I found this friend, closer than my skin.
I call Him Father,
Who is like my Father Friend,
Brother Friend,
Helper Friend.
You need them spirited beyond flesh and blood.
You need them physically and spiritually one with you.
You're strongest with them,
Weakest on your own.

"The situation can get worse and seem hopeless, but with God things will turn out for the best. The only situation I cannot imagine is being without God. Everyone needs a friend, when the going is good and when it's tough. Caroline, you need a friend. Find Him, the best friend ever, the friend who will stick closer than your brother or husband. Make sure you pray a personal prayer of commitment in order to make God your friend."

Caroline smiles. "Thank you so much, Joe, for sharing the poem with me, and for all you've told me this evening. I'm very encouraged that there's hope."

"When is your due date?"

"October 30."

Joe makes a note of that in his diary. "I may be able to come back that week. As I mentioned, I'll be praying for you and will get other friends to pray for you, too. We'll also fast for you. As soon as I go back to school, I shall find a free weekend so my friends and I can come back to have a time of prayer for you and your family. From your story, I reckon that you have wined and dined with the devils, and they will not easily let you go. We need to muster all the weapons of warfare against them. You need deliverance, for those devils will do everything to get their pound of flesh from the spot closest to your heart. Nothing can stop them unless you team up with the One who can stand up to any trouble. He alone has the power to command peace. Let's pray briefly, and then I'll let you go back home to your family before they get worried about you."

They pray that God will help Caroline take the right steps towards returning to Him. Joe allows Caroline to ask God for forgiveness. He then prays that He will protect her from the attacks of the spirit-woman.

"Please bid your mother good night for me. I need to be on my way," Caroline says as she gets up to leave. She has so much on her mind that she is unable to stop for another chat with Mama Joe.

"I'll definitely tell her. You don't need to thank me. This is our battle. Greet your family." He escorts her to the gate, opens it, and bids her good night.

CHAPTER THIRTY-FOUR

By the time Caroline reaches home, Onyema is back already. Caroline begins to have misgivings about discussing her mission to Mama Joe's house. She's not sure what he will think. She's not given to lying to her husband, and she has no choice but to tell him where she was. Without waiting for him to ask, she tells him the truth.

"But why? It's been a long time you visited there," Onyema says half in protest.

"With the threats on my life and that of our baby, I thought it would be wise to confide in Joe."

"Okay, so...?"

"Joe is better able to understand me, given his encounter with Ogwugwu."

Onyema remains silent.

"I'm sorry for not telling you," she says. "It's necessary for me to seek support, for the good of us all."

"That's okay. I'm not upset, but you should have informed me," Onyema says. "So, what did he do for you?"

She looks down. "He asked me to pray and invite God into my life so He can take care of my situation."

Onyema is uncomfortable with the suggestion, but he feels he must welcome any suggestion that will contribute to their safe landing from the current tightrope.

"Will you do it?" Onyema inquires.

"I think I will. I also think it's high time that I determine my stand about God and this whole issue of faith. I've been looking for quick fixes without making any serious commitment." Caroline looks at Onyema with imploring eyes, yearning for understanding and support.

"You know I love you and I'm ready to do anything to keep you safe," he tells her. "If God will deliver you, I will be open to knowing who He is and making a commitment to Him. But one thing is sure: I love you and will not stand against what will keep you safe and happy; I promise that."

"Onyi, thank you so much for your understanding. I love you, too."

They hug each other. Onyema holds her in a warm embrace and she begins to weep.

After they send their children to bed, they retire to the bedroom. Their love and understanding warms them and keeps them strong, despite the uncertainty that's threatening to overwhelm them. They are glad to have each other to love and to hold.

Caroline kneels by their bedside and begins to pray. Onyema watches, debating whether or not to join.

Chapter Thirty-Five

Joe kneels by his bedside and begins to pray for Caroline. He understands what it means to be under siege by contrary forces. They are ruthless manipulators, especially when they assume authority over someone. Their rage and tyranny, if unchecked, will not only destroy an individual but continue the destruction for generations. He empathizes with Caroline's pain and asks God to show her mercy. He continues to pray until he senses that he has fully communicated to God his concerns and desires for Caroline's wellbeing.

Mama is surprised but impressed with Caroline's honesty and humility. Caroline knows how to get the help she needs when she needs it. Even though it has been more than a year since Caroline last visited, she still felt confidence that she would receive support from them. Joe shares his burden for Caroline's wellbeing so that his mother can support by praying regularly also.

Once in a while, Brother Goodnews visits Joe at the university to share with him some principles of spiritual warfare, and to pray with him. Having discerned that Joe loves God and wants to do great things for God, Goodnews sends him materials on discipleship. Through discipleship, he believes that Joe's future as a minister of God will be secured.

From the interactions Joe has with experienced Gospel ministers, he continues to learn and grow. He learns the power of corporate anointing, because two are better than one and iron sharpens iron. He understands the synergy of unity and knows that he has to live his life prepared, in active engagement with God, to discern the best course of action in any given situation. The elders say that the person who goes into battle hastily doesn't know that a battle is tantamount to death.

"A wise warrior is better than a strong one," Brother Goodnews reminds him one day, quoting from Proverbs 24, "and a man of knowledge is better than one of strength. You should wage war with sound guidance. Victory comes with many counsellors."

Joe is determined to be thorough in dealing with Caroline's case, for he knows what it means for a soldier to be wounded in a battle. The spirit woman may go to any lengths to execute vengeance on Caroline, because she considers Caroline a renegade. Her agenda—poverty and wretchedness for Caroline's family through control and manipulation—is being cut short as Caroline begins to think for herself.

On returning to school, Joe calls together some of his close friends and associates from the outreach team and tells them Caroline's story. He asks for their support in praying for her. He also asks them to consider the possibility of joining him in visiting the village next month in order to pray for Caroline and her family.

Four members of the team volunteer to go with him—Peter, Maxwell, Ify, and Monica. Three of them are able to travel together with Joe, but not Monica. She will join them later, as she needs to travel from Mbia. They plan to arrive on a Friday evening and then meet with Caroline and her family on Saturday. They will return to school on Sunday afternoon.

Mama makes provisions for their lodging and meals. They eat African salad as an appetizer. It consists of grated cassava chips with oil bean seeds, dried fish, garden eggplant and leaves, onions, pepper, and fresh palm oil. They enjoy the food, but eat cautiously because they know Mama will still treat them to a main dish later in the evening. They unwind from their journey, eating cherries from the shrubs used to line the walls. They also eat red and yellow cashew fruit from the numerous trees. It's a nice break from their hectic campus lives of constant study, Christian fellowship activities, and hasty meals.

Mama, as the generous hostess, spoils them with sumptuous appetizers, desserts, and homemade orange juice. They wait for Monica, who is supposed to arrive at 6:00, but she is late. They decide to eat dinner without her. For the main course, they have yam porridge with dry fish and chicken. It is a welcome feast and they are very appreciative.

Before retiring for the night, they talk briefly about their plans for the next day. Joe confirms that Caroline and her family are expecting them. They close with an intense but brief prayer. The prayer is fervent, oozing the passion of young people on a mission to gain audience with the great King. Monica still hasn't arrived when they finish, so they pray for her and retire to their bedrooms in the hopes that she will still be able to join them by the morning.

Mama shows them to their rooms. The big bungalow is built to provide comfortable accommodations for the family, and also to have enough rooms for visitors. Two guest bedrooms, which share a bathroom, are situated at the north side of the bakery, a bit separate from the rest of the bedrooms. Peter and Maxwell share one room, as it contains two double beds. Ify sleeps in the second room alone.

They tidy up and retire, thankful for the comfort of a house that meets their needs.

Gradually, everyone drifts off to sleep. Saturday will be busy and they will be fasting for most of the day.

Joe is worried about Monica even though he plays down his fear of something bad happening to her. He's puzzled as to what might have made it impossible for her to join them that evening and into the night. He's restless, wondering why she has not come, and concerned about her safety. He decides to pray some more for her.

Since the others have joined him here at his insistence, he feels responsible for their safety. All of them love Monica, because she is such an amiable young lady. She cares for everyone like a mother; they call her "MM," meaning Mummy Me. She is one of the youngest in the group, but she takes responsibility to ensure that everyone is comfortable and happy. Joe loves to chat with her because she's a sensible young lady who can speak her mind when necessary yet sound pleasant doing it.

Finally, at midnight, he ends his vigil—or rather, sleep overtakes him.

His sleep is interrupted when he dreams that Monica is standing outside his door, knocking. He staggers to his feet and proceeds to open the door. Only then does he realize he is actually dreaming.

The dream was so vivid that he doesn't immediately go back to sleep. He sits on the edge of his bed listening for something—perhaps a knock or any sound to confirm or refute his vision. He prays again for Monica's safety, for it is unlike Monica to not show up after giving her word.

CHAPTER THIRTY-SIX

He attempts to go back to bed. Unable to do so, he continues to pray for Monica until 3:00 a.m. He reminds himself that he needs to be physically and spiritually strong in the morning, so he needs to catch some sleep.

His sleep is dreamless and refreshing. By 7:00 a.m., Joe is still sleeping as the sun streams down on him through the window from the parted curtain.

A knock at the door awakes him. He pulls himself up from the bed, then opens the front door. He sees no one, but then the knock comes again and he hears someone call his name. He recognizes the voice and understands the direction of the knock. His room has a connection to an access door that leads outside. It was built that way so one could easily gain entrance when the gate is locked, rather than disturbing the whole house. Only people who are close to the family know about the door.

As Joe opens the door, he sees Monica. He first imagines that it might be a dream, but then Monica calls his name and extends her hand to him. He lets out a shout and lets her in. He embraces her, gathering her in his arms like a shepherd carrying a lost sheep close to his heart. He holds her that way for some time, feeling relieved to see her.

The others rush out of their guest rooms to see why he shouted. They enter Joe's room and see him locked in an embrace with Monica. They, too, are excited, though also a bit uneasy about the close and prolonged embrace. They express cautious joy at seeing Monica safe and sound. Joe senses the uneasiness of the others; as a group of young men and women, they know friendship, love, and cooperation, but in their relationships with one another they don't explore close physical touch.

"You are most welcome, dear sister," Joe says to Monica. "I'm sure everyone is happy and would like to hear your story. Why were you unable to join us last night?"

"Welcome, my sister," Ify says.

"Sister Monica! Thank God!" Maxwell exclaims.

"We'll hear your story," Peter says. "I'm happy that you're here, safe and sound."

Monica pulls away from Joe. "I thank all of you. I'm so glad to be here. It's a long story, but God is amazing both in good and bad times,"

Joe dismisses everyone by saying, "I better go get ready. Monica, take your bag and make yourself comfortable with Ify. We are fasting today, as we agreed, but you can tell Mama if you want to eat breakfast. We'll meet in the smaller parlour by the guest rooms. You can join us later. Take your time, we'll not pressure you."

"Oh no," Monica says. "I've already missed part of the meeting and I don't want to miss more. I'm bursting to tell you all about what happened yesterday."

Monica leaves with Ify, and Maxwell and Peter return to their room.

No one is late for the meeting. Joe starts with the opening prayer, but soon afterwards he allows time for interaction because he knows everyone is curious to hear Monica's story. The buses that travel from Mbia to Ludu don't leave so early on Saturdays.

Monica tells the group about how she left campus on Friday and boarded a bus to Onitsha. The bus driver stopped to fuel and was about to continue the journey when Monica saw a vehicle drive by. She recognized the vehicle as belonging to her eldest brother, Daniel, who lives in Makurdi. She asked the driver to speed up and flag him down. She then joined Daniel in his Peugeot 504 Salon, since he was going home, too. She was very happy at this change in plan since Daniel's car was more comfortable than the crowded bus.

She explained to Daniel that she was travelling home to get money and provisions for the remaining part of the semester. She also informed him that she was supposed to be in Ludu by 6:00 p.m. Her brother knew Joe's house very well since he had once dropped Monica off there for a retreat.

When they were about thirty kilometres to Onitsha, the car developed a problem. He stopped to check the fuel pump. It seemed to be fine, but he noticed some fuel on the engine. When they continued, the car would move a short distance before jerking to a stop.

He was able to get the vehicle to a roadside mechanic, an enthusiastic young fellow who claimed to know exactly what was wrong. He checked to see if the fuel was igniting in the combustion chamber, and then checked the spark plugs, wires, harness, distributor cap, cerebration, and fuel filter. He concluded that he just needed to change the plugs, as they seemed to be dead—and soaked with oil. He got new plugs from his shop and installed them. He also changed the fuel pump. When they tested the vehicle by driving it around the shop, it seemed to be working fine. Relieved, Daniel paid him the fee without haggling and left.

The vehicle worked fine as they continued on their journey. But after ten kilometres, the same problems returned. They managed to drive to another mechanic's workshop. The shop owner wasn't in, but they met his apprentice, who claimed to have learned the trade and offered to take a look.

The apprentice set to work and soon announced that the car had a huge problem: engine knock. This time, Daniel was exasperated and Monica very worried for her schedule, since he had to be in Ludu in an hour.

Finally, another idea struck the young mechanic. He smelled the fuel and announced to Daniel that he had put contaminated fuel in the vehicle. Daniel scratched his head and thought for a while. He remembered buying fuel from a group of fuel hawkers on the lonely stretch of road near Oturkpo. He had debated whether to buy fuel there, but decided to risk it since he was already so low. Speechless, he realized that he himself was to blame.

The mechanic advised him to go to a filling station and drain off the fuel and get clean fuel. They paid him for his time.

By the time they reached a certified gas station, it was already 6:00 p.m. The line-up was long, and Daniel bought several jerry cans in which to store the fuel that was already in his tank. When others confirmed that the fuel was really bad, he decided to drain the fuel completely. Since they had no option, they had to wait in the long queue until about 8:00 p.m. As predicted, the car drove smoothly after that.

"By the time we reached home, it was 9:00," Monica says. "My only option was to sleep in Mbia, but I was just thankful that the day—and our trouble—was over. I was very grateful to God that Daniel and I were safe. Very early in the morning, Daniel drove me to this place."

The others are very happy for Monica's safety, despite the trying journey.

CHAPTER THIRTY-SEVEN

After worship, exhortation, and prayer, they set off for Caroline's house. They are well received and the program begins in earnest. Caroline rededicates her life to Jesus, and Onyema and the children plan to do the same—but Onyema excuses himself, saying that he has another engagement and is unable to participate. Caroline is disappointed, because Onyema didn't mention any engagement to her when she told him about the program.

As soon as he leaves, the program continues. All the children receive prayers to surrender their lives to Christ.

"This is a strong foundation upon which to stand in order to pull down, cast out, and rebuild people's lives for victory," Joe says.

They begin to pray with Caroline to nullify the power, influence, and hold of the spirit woman on her life and household. When Caroline declares that she is breaking the bond between her and the spirit woman, she falls to the ground and turns hostile towards the people praying for her. She pushes their hands away.

Immediately they sense that it is not Caroline doing this; the spirit woman is registering her protest by using Caroline's body. She is trying to distract, intimidate, and fool them into thinking she's too powerful to be put where she belongs. They understand the tactic, especially the fact that their fight isn't against flesh and blood but against principalities, powers, rulers of darkness of this present world, and spiritual wickedness in high places. They cast out the spirit woman and Caroline becomes calm and starts cooperating with them again.

They focus on praying for her, especially that she be strengthened and not discouraged by anything that might come her way. They also pray for her children and husband.

Caroline's joy knows no bounds when they finish. She feels as though a huge load has been lifted from her heart. She is ecstatic and energized. They counsel and instruct her from the Bible, and are about to leave when Onyema returns. On seeing how happy, relaxed, and confident Caroline looks and feels, as well as the children, he regrets not taking part in the meeting. He thanks them profusely and they encourage him to give God a chance in his life, too.

Afterward Joe and his friends return to Joe's house, where Mama has prepared sumptuous pounded yam and soup made with leaves of gnetum Africanum. However, rather than eat, they go into praise and intercessory prayers until 7:00 p.m. They then eat their supper with joy and ease of mind.

They spend the evening visiting with Mama and Joe's other siblings and are set to go back to school after the morning service at Mama's church. Mama hands a bag of goodies to each of them. She has prepared chop-one-chop-two and plantain chips to last them a while at school, especially as they're starting their exam season soon. They cannot thank her enough for her kindness and support.

For some reason, Mama takes a special interest in Monica, giving her extra provisions and money. She finds Monica to be a very down-to earth young woman. Even though the whole team works together and are friendly with one another, she notices that there seems to be a close attachment between Monica and her son. They are both disciplined young people who are safe with one another. What more could she wish than for her son to be surrounded by good companions so that together they can sharpen one another as iron?

CHAPTER THIRTY-EIGHT

Caroline goes from counting weeks to counting days for the delivery of her baby. Every premonition seems to have disappeared. The happy and confident couple continues to work hard and enjoy their lives. Caroline packs for the maternity ward, since labour can start at any time.

On the night of October 30, as Caroline is sleeping, she hears a voice sneer at her from out of the darkness.

"Wise woman, what do you think you are doing? You are only deceiving yourself if you think that anything or anybody can deliver you out of my hands. For taking steps that are contrary to our relationship, tonight your life and that of your baby will be sacrificed to atone for the sabotage you dared bring upon my kingdom." The spirit woman sighs, shooting out a breath of air. "Make no mistake about this. Tonight, upon my altar, your blood and your baby's must be spilled. We shall drink in the blood! Mark my words, foolish woman! We'll meet and know who has the final word in this matter."

Peels of echoing laughter ravage Caroline with fear.

Caroline suddenly sees a vision of her body helplessly jolting back and forth. She sees her body dangling before her, utterly wretched, like a ripped basket carried by waves on a turbulent sea. Caroline is physically shaken as the laughter fills the room.

Confused, she imagines that she's having a very bad dream. Then Onyema shakes her, asking, "Why is your body trembling in this way? What is wrong?"

Caroline opens her eyes to see him sitting beside her, staring closely into her face.

Suddenly, the laughter stops. She is confused; the voice sounded initially like that of the spirit woman. Has she dreamed it?

"Did you hear the laughter?" she whispers softly.

"No, I didn't. But it seemed as though somebody just left the room."

Caroline then tells him of the threats she heard from the enraged voice. The couple is badly shaken, and surprised that the battle is not yet over with their tormentor. This is beyond what they can humanly contain.

They are filled of confusing thoughts. What will they do? Caroline's solution is to pray and scream out her prayers at the top of her lungs so as to ease the agitation on her mind.

Caroline wants to pray together with Onyema, but she's unable to suggest it to him. They have never prayed together, so it would be awkward to begin now, in the midst of their confusion. She can neither weep nor talk, because her thoughts are running in different directions, like dust blown about by a violent wind.

While the voice she heard unmistakably came from the spirit woman, the distortion made it more terrifying and unearthly than ever. It was saturated with anger and vengeance.

Onyema gets up to light a lantern. "What do you want to do?"

"Pray," she answers simply.

Onyema is surprised. He has seen her sometimes kneeling beside their bed, or in the living room with the children, but she hasn't been in the habit of inviting him to pray with her. He doesn't appreciate why in such a serious matter her answer is to pray. But if prayer will help, why not try it?

"You can pray if you wish," he says, sighing with an aching heart.

Caroline prays a simple prayer: "Oh God, You are merciful and compassionate. I have made You my friend. Please come to me at this hour of desperation. I don't know where to turn, but I am turning to You. You can help me out of this danger. Please help protect my baby. Be our refuge. Make us strong to fight this battle and win it in Jesus' name. I thank You for Your help and support. Amen."

Onyema echoes "Amen," surprised at the simplicity of her prayer.

They don't know whether to wish for sleep or stay awake. Both remember that she's already due for her baby to be delivered.

Caroline soon drifts into sleep and Onyema is surprised at the soundness of her sleep. He watches her breathing to assure himself that she is fine and only sleeping. He watches her for one hour, refusing to sleep until his weary eyes close against his will. He catches himself falling asleep and wards it off by shaking his head vigorously. He makes an effort to keep awake by thinking about the events of the night. He checks the time and sees that it is 1:30 a.m. Moments later, sleep returns to his eyes. He lies down on the bed and softly lifts Caroline's head, resting it on his outstretched left arm. He rests the other arm lightly over her breast to make sure she is comfortable. He shows the determination of a husband who is ready to do anything to protect his wife and unborn baby. He breathes softly to make sure he doesn't disturb the peaceful sleep that has overcome her. Soon he, too, drifts off to sleep.

CHAPTER THIRTY-NINE

Caroline is traveling with her family in a Mercedes Benz. Her husband is driving and she's sitting in the passenger's seat, with their three children in the back. The scenery is familiar to her, for they often travelled around the country this way in the past. Even though the road looks familiar, she's not sure of where they're going. Unexpectedly, they hear a noise and the car starts to swerve. Her husband manages to control the car and bring it to a stop. It is a burst tire, and they all need to get out so he can change it. Because she's pregnant, she carefully lifts herself out of her seat.

As soon as she's out of the vehicle, her surroundings get very dark. Lights glitter in the distance and she finds herself heading towards the light, moving very fast, as though she has wings. She cannot understand herself why she's leaving her family in this lonely place.

She trips and lands in the dirt with a thud, on her stomach with her hands outstretched.

"Oh my baby," she groans, clutching her tummy.

She rolls to her side and lies there helpless for some minutes. Everything looks hazy. Promptly, she notices a pair of huge eyes staring at her. Then she passes out and remembers nothing.

She is brought back to the consciousness by a very scary voice that makes her shiver with fear.

"Hello," the voice whispers. "I have been waiting for you. I've been planning for this meeting since I observed your waywardness in challenging my authority. I want to meet with you beyond the walls of your home so that you shall know me fully and what I stand for."

Laughter fills the voice. Even the surroundings seem to vibrate with the laughter.

"There's no time to wasted," she says, the metallic laughter stopping abruptly. "We shall settle our differences today, which will mark your end—and, of course, your stupidity. You think that my gifts are for nothing. You cannot receive my help and keep your soul at the same time."

Recognition creeps upon Caroline immediately. The voice belongs to the spirit woman. A quiver goes through her body. She needs no further confirmation as to what this is about.

She hears footsteps behind her, but she dares not turn her head. She doesn't want to find out what other death messengers are coming for her.

Something taps her on the shoulder, and two voices whisper in unison: "Finally she is here. This is going to be exciting. We shall have a good meal."

She tries to convince herself that she might not have heard them right. She holds her breath.

"It's been a while since I last tasted fresh blood," a shrill female voice says. "The best of the feast is to bite the neck and suck the blood from there." She smacks her tongue as though already tasting the fresh blood.

It's too late to regret anything, Caroline encourages herself. *I must plan my escape. But how?*

The reality hits her. She seems to be in in the territory of her attackers, with no help or room for escape. She considers praying, but her thoughts are too scattered. She thinks about springing to her feet and challenging them, but she imagines that will be useless. She doesn't even know how many creatures are present.

They poke her side with a sharp object, probably a prong, or a dagger. Caroline loses every hope for escape. Wounded, she makes her last wishes to whoever will care to listen or take note.

"Agnes, didn't you say you wanted to suck the blood?" a man's voice says sharply. "Why are you wasting it?"

Caroline remembers that the spirit woman once told her that her name is Agnes, but that she should never call her by name

This is it, she thinks. *Agnes has planned this revenge to kill both me and my baby. It's useless to beg her. This will be our end.*

"I want the damned beast to wake up and be alert. I hate to bite her neck while she's in a coma-like state. I enjoy the way the blood pumps when they're awake and alert. Their plea for mercy is like an appetizer. Nobody ever receives mercy here. Mercy is with Him who lives in the third heavens, not in this epitome of wickedness."

The coven echoes with the crackling peels of Agnes's laughter.

Another poke and a rough jerk, and then Caroline is on her feet. Two piercing eyes look her full in the face. She uses her left hand to shield her eyes from the brightness of a nearby blazing fire. Skulls hang on the wall as decoration.

She feels a bite on two fingers of her left hand, which she has raised to her face. Her two fingers must be gone. She notices that Agnes is chewing something.

"I swear, this is going to be delicious. The bones are succulent and full of marrow," Agnes says, smacking her lips. Her eyes gleam with relish.

Agnes is a witch, a murderer, the deadliest demon, a witch of the highest order, she thinks. *But what does it matter now? If she were Lucifer himself, nothing could change my fate. Doom is inevitable.*

Caroline pictures herself and her unborn baby as meat in the stomach of deadly vultures.

"I will have the other three fingers before you bite off the neck," a man says. "We shall take turns sucking the blood."

"No," a woman protests. "I was the one who sent my errand demon to obstruct their way and distract her to follow the light. Agnes, you shall be content with what I give you to eat. I shall share only what I want to share!"

There are probably three creatures here, Caroline thinks. *There is Agnes, then her male partner, and this new female voice that I just heard.*

Her emotions change from terror to horror, from despondency to suicide. She concludes that her life is done. These hellish creatures will not eat her and her unborn baby, then tear them limb from limb, the most painful death possible.

Abruptly, she resolves to fight. *If I must die, I will not die like a coward to agents of darkness. I have suffered violations from these forces, but I resolve to take my freedom by force.*

Her resolve numbs her fear and pain. She remembers what one of them said, that mercy is with Him who lives in the third heavens. She remembers the prayers and biblical instructions Joe gave her. She remembers 2 Corinthians 10:3–6. She remembers that Joe had warned her that her enemy would not easily let up; she would regroup and involve like-minded spirits after the defeat meted out to her on that eventful Saturday. She would attack in the fiercest way, just to see if she could plant doubt and erode Caroline's confidence.

Joe and his group warned her to always enforce her new authority over forces that are contrary to her wellbeing, no matter the situation. Demons are agents of Satan, and she need not fear them, for greater is He that is in her than he that is working in them.

Energy and determination well up inside her. Instantly, she steps back and spits on the ground to indicate her utter revulsion. She looks in the direction of Agnes and stares into the witch's face. Agnes's face is frightening to behold. It is covered with red and black marks. She looks haggard and wears a gaudy gown with open shoulders. Her eyes are sharp, penetrating, disarming, and confident.

Locked in eye-to eye combat, Caroline is determined not to die like a coward. Her face is set like flint, glossy and ready to rain fire. For months she has endured torment, frustration, and disappointment. She spits again on the ground.

"This cannot be true," two voices say together. "Is she His? Nobody has ever desecrated our sanctuary by spitting on our sacred ground. Abomination!"

By showing that she is unafraid, Caroline has confused them. They can see that she, too, has powers.

Let them wonder where my confidence stems from, she thinks. *What a blessing! I belong to Him.*

She finally addresses them in their confusion. "Listen, if you don't know already, I belong to Jesus. God can deliver me from your hands, you wicked spirits. I played into your hands, but the One who dwells in the third heavens shows me mercy and delivers me. I ask Him to whom mercy belongs to protect me now, in Jesus's name. I scatter your plans and pull down your stronghold. I nullify your claim over me. The blood of Jesus covers my baby and I declare—"

She is cut short when her surroundings change abruptly. Lightning flashes through the room and the creatures fall, covering their heads with their hands and shouting gibberish. They writhe on the floor as though stricken with violent pain.

Caroline locates the exit, but her way is blocked by something on the floor. She stops. When she tries to move again, she bumps her head against an invisible wall and falls backward. She gets up again, feeling dizzy. She begins to pray—commanding, binding, and resisting—surprisingly energized. She must fight for her life, even if she dies in the process.

Her strength comes back to her, but she must act fast.

She begins to run, moving as fast as she can, even though it feels at times like she's going in circles. To her relief, she discovers that she is making progress, but her feet are heavy. Miraculously, without knowing where she is going, she finally breaks through the darkness to where her family has fallen asleep inside the car.

As she tries to wake them, she hears footsteps hurrying towards her. The sound of laughter and murmurs get closer and louder.

She checks the date and time on her wristwatch. Behold, it is 3:30 a.m., October 31.

She closes her eyes and speaks with determination. "I am alive and free, no matter what they think. I have overcome!"

When she opens her eyes, she sees her husband, next to her sleeping. She closes her eyes again, wondering where she is. She reaches out and shakes Onyema, trying to wake him up.

"Let's go home," she says. "We have won! We are safe. I will not die, even though I'm wounded."

———

"Caroline? Open your eyes." In bed, Onyema pleads with his wife to wake up. Caroline is delirious and speaking incoherently. "We are home in our house. Which home are we going to? Who has wounded you? Talk to me."

He quickly gets dressed and rushes her to the hospital in their old Datsun. When they arrive, he's unable to tell the nurses what the problem is.

"Caroline, is this how you will leave me, when our lives seem to be coming together again?" he says. "Please, please don't leave me. Come back."

This couple must have lost their minds, the sleepy nurse imagines. *Either that or they are fighting a grim battle to the death.*

The commotion continues for a while. Other night workers come out to watch while Caroline, without opening her eyes, continues to mutter about her victory and safety. Her husband cries and pleads for help. He knows something has gone wrong.

The nurses set to work, trying to calm him down so they can get some kind of history before calling in the doctor.

Caroline becomes tired and slips into a coma.

When the doctor arrives, he assesses the situation. He must decide whether to carry out a Caesarean Section on an unconscious woman. Finally, he decides to perform the procedure, for Caroline's water has broken. They must hope to save the life of the baby and fight for the life of the mother once the baby is delivered.

The nurses worry that Caroline will not survive, because she does not regain consciousness before the surgery.

Onyema sends words for Joe to come straight to the hospital. Joe arrives with two other friends shortly before Caroline is wheeled out of the theatre into the recovery room. During the surgery, not even Onyema was allowed in the operating room; he was left to wander the corridor.

To everyone's great relief, they learn that the Caesarean Section has been successful. Caroline has given birth to a healthy baby girl who weighs four and half kilograms.

Afterword

Caroline and Onyema began a new life with the birth of their fourth child. Onyema's revived passion for his wife, found and polished in the crucible of overwhelming trouble, never waned. Love empowered him to work hard for his family to meet their needs. He went on to attend church and become an associate minister. His love and concern for others grew and he became a great leader in his home and in the community. The couple decided to relocate to Abuja, where they set up their import business of clothing and home accessories. Caroline opened a high-end boutique, selling fashionable styles. Their dream of flourishing financially came true.

Joe became a lawyer and an associate pastor in his church. He married Monica, his university sweetheart, with whom he shared a vision to liberate communities and even nations.

Mama Joe died at a very good age of 101. Before she died, her memory remained intact. Her limbs didn't badly deteriorate, and she was still strong enough to assist in making meals. She continued to cook the best meals in the house until after her one hundredth birthday. Gradually, Monica became the mommy of the house as all the girls got married and left home. Jonathan became independent as a medical doctor and married another doctor.

Later in life, Joe wrote a poem for all the women in his life. It was written in honour of his mother and the courage of her life, for she had the perfect blend of physical and spiritual strength.

Good woman, max charms by unshackling your mindset.
Sell your coat and buy a sword.
Into those tender gums let sharp fangs fit,
Biting and cutting in submission.
Your delicate sole must crush stones sent to dethrone.
Your bosom, tender with love and purpose,
Must wield the weapon expertly.
Your tender hands must handle a rose and a sword.
Your luscious lips must squeeze,
Squirt spirit, sword, and smoke.

The Lion-Lamb leads you to war.
You are a wise serpent and innocent dove,
All in one body dwell.
Great human, sell your skirt and buy a sword.
Possess your kingdom or be exiled.

Your God, mighty and terrible in battle,
Fights lawfully and not forcefully.
His enemies, confused, destroy themselves.
Your battle He fights,
Not with weapons of hate and false hope.

Steel love set in the deep sea of forgiveness,
Affluent in patience and deep in judgment.
He executes justice and mercy.
Fight not for Him but abide.
Move Him, for you cannot run from this warrior of justice.

Index of Traditional First Names and Their Meanings

Afamefuna: My name lives on.

Ifeyinwa: Nothing is as precious as a child.

Ikeaza: One who responds with strength.

Neme: Performer.

Nkeiruka: The future is greater than the past.

Nnamdi: My father lives.

Nneka: Mother is supreme.

Nwakaego: A child is more precious than wealth.

Nwokenku: Literarily means "Woodman," but it refers to a strong or resilient man.

Obianujunwa: The one born in the midst of other children.

Obinna: The father's heart.

Odiba: To overlook issues.

Ogochukwu: God's kindness.

Onyema (Chukwu): Who knows the mind of God?

Ositadinma: It gets better from this point.

PIDGIN ENGLISH TRANSLATION
(CHAPTER EIGHT)

Still smiling, he holds the gate open. "It's good to see you, Madam. Long time no see."

"It's good to see you too, Yang."

"How is your family?" he asks.

"We're well. How is your family?"

"We're fine, except that we're hungry. What did you bring for me?"

Caroline mimics his sad tone of voice. "I didn't bring you any gift because hunger is everywhere."

"Ah, Madam, it's because you don't like me. Even the least present is better than nothing."

"Oh no. Why wouldn't I like you? You're a good man. I'll not forget to bring a present for you next time."

"You said so yourself, so I would remind you," he says. "You're a lucky woman, for my master just came back. He had left for a meeting early in the morning."

"Yes, of course, I'm a lucky woman. Thank you."